D0407086

NO LONGER PROPERTY OF
ANYTHINK LIBRARIES/
RANGEVIEW LIBRARY DISTRICT

Far

from

Normal

BECKY WALLACE

PAGE STREET
PUBLISHING CO.

PAGE STREET
PUBLISHING CO.

Copyright © 2020 Becky Wallace

First published in 2020 by
Page Street Publishing Co.
27 Congress Street, Suite 105
Salem, MA 01970
www.pagestreetpublishing.com

All rights reserved. No part of this book may be reproduced or used, in any form
or by any means, electronic or mechanical, without prior permission in writing
from the publisher.

Distributed by Macmillan, sales in Canada by The Canadian Manda Group.

24   23   22   21   20   1   2   3   4   5

ISBN-13: 978-1-6456-0-568
ISBN-10: 1-6456-0-562

Library of Congress Control Number: 201995 7091

Cover and book design by Rosie Stewart for Page Street Publishing Co.
Cover illustrations: girl © Shutterstock / NotionPic; boy © Shutterstock / IfH;
dog © Shutterstock / Macrovector; skyline © Shutterstock / Norvan Screen

Printed and bound in the United States

Page Street Publishing protects our planet by donating to nonprofits
like The Trustees, which focuses on local land conservation.

FOR GAVIN, LAYNIE, AUDREY, AND ADY.

I've made up hundreds of fake people, but you four are my greatest creations. Love you always.

One

I LOVE CHICAGO. IT'S LITERALLY MY FAVORITE PLACE IN THE world—except in the summer when it's full of tourists. You can't go anywhere without running into one of those annoying, slow-walking, selfie-taking fanny-pack wearers. And for the last several summers, I've been one of them. Minus the fanny-pack wearing part because even though they're on trend, my grandma doesn't leave the house without hers, and I love Grammy, but refuse to dress like her.

As I stand outside 900 North Michigan Avenue, head tilted back to take in the beautiful gray stone building with its four castle-like towers, I realize that even without the typical attire, I probably still look like a tourist.

Not today, Chicago. Not today.

I tug down the hem of the little black dress I misappropriated from my aunt's closet, make sure no one saw me gawking, and stride into the building's side entrance with all the purpose I can muster. That's where the employees who work in the building's upper levels check in. The security machine issues a happy little beep as I scan my first real work badge and head to the elevators with a slew of other professionals, young and otherwise.

My wedge heels skid as they hit the metal grating just inside the elevator, but I recover fast. No one says *anything* to me, which is exactly what I want because that means I'm blending in. I don't look like a seventeen-year-old who's interning with her aunt for the summer.

By the time I reach the twenty-seventh floor, it's just me and my reflection. Even wavy and oddly tinted in the elevator door, I like what I see. With my hair down and Aunt Emma's dress on, I look like I belong in Chicago.

A new Maddie. A better Maddie. A Maddie no one expects to fail.

The doors open onto a reception area painted the perfect shade of orange. It's not too bright or too brown, an impeccable backdrop for the giant, stylized *V* that fills the space like artwork. Velocity Marketing has a cool vibe to match its reputation.

I bet Aunt Emma chose the design for the office. She's got the best aesthetic—and the reputation to match. I never would have put a lavender couch and a faux-fur rug into a Lincoln Park penthouse apartment, but she's got vision.

Let's hope it extends to me too.

Putting on my most confident smile, I approach the desk. "Hi! You must be Patty. I've heard great things about you. I'm Maddie McPherson, the new intern."

Patty's super thick, painted-on eyebrows rise. "Oh yes." She nods a few times, eyes raking over me, before continuing. "I've heard *all* about you too. I'll call William to take you back to training."

What could she have possibly heard? I mean, I had to apply for this internship just like anyone else. Emma surely put in a good word for me, but something about Patty's tone makes the yogurt I ate for breakfast sour in my stomach.

"Great," I say, trying to sound more enthusiastic than nervous. Some kids at my high school wear these plastic WWJD bracelets, but right now, I'm wondering less about what Jesus would do and more what Emma might. I clear my throat and try to engage Patty in conversation: "Is that your dog?" I ask, pointing to the framed photo at the end of her desk.

"Umm-hmm." She ignores my effort and her bright pink fingernails continue clicking across the keyboard.

"He's really cute. I mean, I'm assuming he's a he. The spiked collar sorta made me think—"

"William is on his way," she says without looking up from her screen.

Oh. Okay. I'll just stop talking now. I have a bad habit of babbling when I'm nervous. Emma offered to bring me into the office today and introduce me to everyone, but I didn't think that would give a great first impression. I'm here to prove that I can stand on my own, that I can be successful without having to be babysat by my super-busy, super-talented aunt.

"Thank you, Patty," I say, pretending she's busy and not plain rude.

A door behind Patty's desk swings open, startling me. It's cleverly hidden so you can't see the seams unless you're looking, and the *V* breaks in half to move with it. It's almost something out of a spy movie. And when a good-looking, dark-haired guy with a stubbly chin and a black button-down shirt walks out, I wonder if I'm about to be inducted into MI6 or the NSA or whatever. The fact that his pants have a silvery sheen, though, kills the whole fantasy for me. They'd look okay onstage or at a ballroom dance competition, but for the office? Nope.

He holds out his hand. "Hi. I'm William. You must be Coffee."

"What? No," I say with a half laugh. "I'm Maddie."

Patty snorts.

William gives my hand a solid shake before turning back

without any explanation or direction. I hesitate for a heartbeat then follow him before the secret door slams shut.

No top-secret weapons or retina scanners wait for me on the other side. Two banks of cubicles flank a narrow walkway. Polite voices float over the textured half-walls, buzzing with more noise than you would have guessed from the reception area.

"All of the other interns have already had their training, so you'll have to jump in with both feet," William says as he strides toward one of the offices that line the building's outer wall—no view of the lake from this side. "We have a hierarchy of assignments. I'm sure your aunt gave you the breakdown of how this all works."

I'm not sure exactly what "all" he's talking about, but if he means that I will do a ton of grunt work in return for a sparkling letter of recommendation and a tiny stipend at the end of the summer, then sure. I guess I know how it works.

I wish for the millionth time that my mom would have let me skip the last few days of school so I could have started on Monday like everyone else. But since she wasn't super supportive of me spending the summer in Chicago, I had to make some concessions.

A girl leans out of the cubicle closest to William's office, eyes wide behind glasses with enormous frames.

He points to her. "For the first couple of days, you'll shadow Intern. Then, if we discover something you're good at, we'll find an assignment for you." He turns to face me once he crosses the threshold of his office, blocking me from following. "And now, I need coffee. Two sugars and a dash of hazelnut creamer."

And then he shuts his door in my face.

I stand there staring at the brown wood, mouth half-open. What the actual hell?

I'm pretty sure I didn't say that out loud, but the girl with the huge glasses answers me like I had.

"They burn through a lot of interns around here. He doesn't bother learning anyone's names until they've stuck around for more than a few weeks." She's wearing one of those chunky cardigans that looks like it was hand-knitted and has her blond hair piled in a messy bun right on top of her head. She's pretty in that effortlessly nerdy way. "He's actually a good guy once you get to know him."

Doubtful. "Okay . . ." I hesitate, shifting my weight from one wedge to the other. *Remember: What would Emma do?* I ask myself. *Be decisive. Act!* "Is there a break room or something around here?" I ask, looking down the hallway that seems to consist of nothing but gray cubicles.

"The kitchen's just around the corner. You'll smell it before you see it. I'll run you through the basics when you come back." Her desk phone rings, but she pauses and says, "I'm Katie, by the way."

"It's nice to meet you. I'm Maddie," I whisper as she picks up the phone. She points toward the kitchen and gives me an encouraging grin.

After the third or fourth bank of cubicles, the hall makes a sharp turn, and the fragrance of burnt coffee and copy machine toner reaches my nose. The kitchen is a gray tunnel so narrow that I could touch both walls at once, and I do, just 'cause I can. A basket of fruit and packaged treats sit on a sideboard at the back of the room next to a water cooler.

As the coffee brews, I tap my fingers on the white countertop and consider my options. I need to give William a reason to remember my name. A *positive* reason.

There's a forgotten pen on the counter, and I use it to give myself a quick tattoo. In big, block letters, I write WWED on the inside of my left wrist.

In this case, I can guess the answer.

I put William's coffee in the only cup with a matching saucer, peel open a chocolate-dipped biscotti, and lay it at an angle behind the mug. Nothing too fancy, given the scant selection in the kitchen, but it looks better than a Styrofoam cup with coffee sloshing over the side.

William's office door is open when I get back, so I set my offering on his desk and smile.

He looks at the cup, then up at me, bushy eyebrows peaked. "Did you need something?"

I think a "thank you" might be in order. "No. I was just . . . do *you* need anything else?"

"I'll let you know when I do. Go see Intern. She has assignments for you First Years."

There's no questioning the derision in his tone. Being a "First Year" must not being a good thing.

"Yes. Thank you. Okay. Bye." I grimace as I walk out of the office, shutting the door after me. Did I thank him and tell him goodbye? Speak sentences, Mads. Or say nothing at all.

Intern—I mean, Katie—is leaning out of her cubicle, chair tilted back as far as it can possibly go without tipping over, and has a giant phone pinched between her shoulder and ear. "Ignore him." She pushes a couple of buttons on the phone before she hangs up. We play a quick round of get to know you. Katie's almost eighteen but will be a senior in the fall, too. Her parents held her back before kindergarten because her birthday is late, and she was really small for her age.

I don't mean to notice, but she's still pretty teeny.

"Your desk will be between mine and Arman's. He's an adorable cupcake of a second-year intern. You'll love him." She ushers me into a cubicle that is identical to hers, complete with a rolling chair, an L-shaped desk, and a blank calendar. "We'll check out a laptop and get you all logged into the system." She points to the cubicle directly across from mine. "That's where Mara sits; she's a third-year, shiny black hair, thinks she's in charge. Javi is another second-year, worshipper of Mara, spends more time in her cube than in his own. They're all doing Big Important Things, but I'll try to introduce you at the end of the day. If you're lucky, you'll only have to associate with them in small doses."

"That bad, huh?"

Katie gives me a dramatic eye roll. "Feel free to make your own judgments." She tugs a paper box out from under her desk and offers it to me, before pulling out a second box for herself. Both are filled to the brim with tabloids from all over the world.

"We'll spend half our time combing through gossip magazines and news articles looking for dirt on Velocity's clients. Sometimes it's boring stuff—like stories in trade magazines—but other times," she pauses to point at a shirtless actor on the cover of one magazine, "other times, it's stuff like *this*."

The headline reads, "I've Made a Lot of Bad Choices," but eating carbs must not have been among them. Dude's got abs for days.

I follow Katie to what she calls the Ugly Conference Room. It's got a big glass-topped table, some rolling chairs, a whiteboard, and a narrow window overlooking the parking garage.

She places folders labeled Bad, Good, and Neutral at the table's center with a stack of sticky tabs and a handful of highlighters. "Let me explain what we're doing, then you can tell me *all* about you while we work."

We've been tasked with digging for stories on some baseball player from Texas who may or may not have thrown a garbage can lid through a restaurant window after he caught his British actress girlfriend kissing her costar.

He totally did it, by the way.

Any mention of the athlete is sorted into one of the files for an executive to review later.

"Major corporations, professional sports teams, and agents hire Velocity to help keep their 'assets viable'—those are William's words, not mine. There's a lot of brand management and event planning stuff." She plucks the top off a highlighter, running it over the baseball player's name. "The image cleanup branch is handled mostly by your aunt. If she can make athletes look like decent humans, or at least not caught up in a scandal, they're more likely to end up on commercials and billboards and endorsing products."

"Which means more money for everyone."

Katie has a giant, sparkly smile with movie-star-white teeth. "Exactly." She kicks back in her chair, feet on the table, magazine in her lap. "Tell me about you and why you're stuck here for the summer."

I give Katie the basic rundown of my life—this is my first time away from home, I actually *want* to work for Velocity when I graduate from college, I love contemporary dance and cake—and she tells me all about training for a triathlon, growing up in the city, and more of the backstory on the three other interns. Each of them is assigned to report directly to one of the executives. They each have "real" assignments, while we're stuck with the leftovers.

"If we don't do anything important, how are we supposed to use this for college applications?" I need to do something impressive so that William can write me a glowing letter of recommendation that will help me get early admission to the University of North Carolina—the starting point for the rest of my life.

She shrugs. "What I gathered from Mara, assignments develop throughout the summer. She says you have to jump on any opportunity that is tossed your way."

I can do that. I'll find something to pounce on.

Something about Katie's tone, and the fact that her feet are on the table, makes me think that this internship might not mean as much to her as it does to me. Which I guess is good. If Katie's not a *pouncer*, then I'll be more likely to score a noteworthy project.

Katie keeps up running commentary as she flips through the magazines, pausing every now and then to show me some dress or gasp at some new celebrity coupling.

"Living your life like this must suck," she says, as she flashes me an article titled "Cellulite before Twenty-Five!" "Of course, you can also afford to have any fat sucked out. So maybe it's not so bad."

I grimace and nod at her, running my highlighter over the phrase "steroid-fueled rage," then add the magazine to the negative folder. Things are not looking good for pretty-boy baseball player, and I've only got three hours of experience.

The door to the conference room pops open, and Aunt Emma leads in her giant boxer, Watford. Apparently, everyone dresses casually and can bring their pets on Fridays—one of the perks of working for Velocity and a cool idea unless you're allergic to dander. The dog drops on the floor at my feet, belly up, expecting me to scratch him. I do because even though he's slobbery, he's sort of irresistible.

"How's it coming in here?" Emma adjusts the big bag over her shoulder. Her dark hair is twisted into a fancy knot at the back of her neck. "Anything unexpected?"

I pass her the magazine I'd just marked, and she frowns.

"Has he been accused of using steroids before?" I ask, clicking the highlighter over and over until I realize how nervous it makes me seem. I know there's no grade on how well I've marked a tabloid passage, but delivering coffee and reading garbage magazines isn't going to give me a chance to shine.

"All of the successful baseball players have been, but we definitely don't need the speculation." She sticks the tabloid in her purse instead of the file. "In addition to this snafu, I have some bad news."

I exchange a quick look with Katie, who somehow managed to get her feet off the table and folded under her chair without me even noticing.

"I have to fly to London for an emergency meeting. I hate to leave you alone your first weekend in the city." Emma makes this teeth-gritting expression that's funnier than it is apologetic. "But I also really need you to watch Watford. There's no room in the dog resort, and even if there was, I don't have time to take him."

Watford rolls his body onto my feet with a huff. He's enormous, way bigger than any boxer I've ever seen, and scary looking. Between the giant dog and her fancy apartment building, I'll be perfectly safe. And honestly, it's kind of exciting. I've never been left alone *anywhere*.

"We'll be fine." I wave off her worries.

"Is your mom going to be mad?"

Yes. Absolutely. But I don't say that. "Nah. She leaves me in charge of Cube all the time." Which is true, but she'd never let me babysit my little brother overnight. What my mom doesn't know isn't going to freak her out. Like that I'm getting paid to read tabloids and that I'm wearing a dress that shows more leg than she'd ever be okay with.

"Plus, it's not like she's going to be completely alone," Katie volunteers, shooting me a look out of the corner of her eye. "I can be her point of contact if she needs anything."

Friend status confirmed.

"Great." Emma pulls a bank envelope out of her bag, along with Watford's leash and her bike seat.

"Oh." I take the metal tube out of her hand. "You rode your bike today?"

"Of course. Watty needs his exercise." She throws her arm around my neck for an awkward sit-stand hug. "You can eat at the restaurants in the building. And there's plenty of cash to cover anything else you might need. Consider it payment for taking care of my baby."

She squats down and kisses him square on the mouth, which is disgusting, considering he just finished licking his balls. "You're a good boy, aren't you? Be so sweet for my Maddie. None of this naughty business."

Watford is the chillest dog. It's going to be the easiest weekend ever. I've got money to spend. No supervision and no responsibilities.

How could anything go wrong?

Two

*C*HICAGO IN JUNE IS A GIFT TO ANYONE WILLING TO BRAVE THE frigid winters. The sun doesn't shine on the narrow road on the north side of the building, but it's the perfect temperature in the shade as I unlock Aunt Em's bike. The humidity is low. My hair is frizz-free for once, lying smooth down my back.

People are whizzing along in the bike lane, socks tucked into pants, moving like they know exactly what they're doing. Small problem: I know next to nothing about bikes. I grew out of mine when I was twelve and my legs got too long to ride without bumping into the handlebars, and I haven't been on one since. I'm a little shaky as I walk down the ramp to the bike path that traces Lake Michigan. I have to stop at the bottom of the slope to wipe my sweaty palms on my borrowed dress.

Pausing for a moment to breathe, I send Katie a quick text to thank her for backing me up with Emma. I *am* going to be fine. My family crashes at Emma's apartment for a few weeks every summer. Chicago is practically my second home.

Music blares from the beachfront. There's some sort of event happening with little soccer fields sectioned off in yellow tape. There's even a temporary grandstand with sponsorship posters hung along its supports. Groups of people clump together on the wide concrete stairs that lead down to the beach, enjoying the games and the weather.

On another day, I'd sit on the steps and let the sun shine on me, but I should probably get Watty home.

"You never forget how to ride a bike, right?" I say to the dog.

He tilts his big square head, one ear cocked, like he knows I'm talking to him, but isn't positive what I'm saying. He's adorable despite the underbite and occasional strings of drool.

My dress is flowy enough to fall between my legs, so at least that won't be a problem. My wedges won't be either. I used to ride in flip-flops as a kid. And yet, my lungs are tight as I slide Watford's leash up to my elbow. He knows how to do this, even if I don't.

I swing my leg over the bike and wobble a little before I get both feet on the pedals. I've got this. So what if I haven't ridden a bike in years?

As I pedal along slowly, Watford picks up his pace, trotting beside me with his mouth open. For a dog with floppy jowls, he looks like he's smiling. It's a beautiful day. I'm in one of the most amazing cities in the world. Things are good. I inhale a breath of beachy air—sunblock, sunshine, and sand—and exhale the last of my negative feelings. Perfect.

I've totally got this.

As we move past the grandstand, the soccer fields come into view. Two teams of guys pass a bright orange ball back and forth, and then it bounces a handful of yards from us.

Watford's head whips toward the ball, and then he's off, yanking the bike to the right, and I know I'm in trouble.

"No, Watford! No!" I pull my elbow back, but it's too late. The ledge of the cement steps appear before me. I try to brake, but the bike skids over the first stair. My feet drop off the pedals, flailing for the ground. One pedal catches me in the shin; the front tire hits the next stair. My stomach lurches under my ribs.

And then I'm airborne.

A BRIGHT LIGHT HANGS ABOVE ME, BLOTTED OUT BY FOUR SHADOWS. Glorious shadows. The kind of arms and shoulders and abs that you only see in magazines or dream about. So, I'm pretty sure I'm dead and this is heaven.

Huh. The Greeks were right. Yay for the pantheon.

"Are you okay?" One of the gods drops down into the sand beside me.

Weird that they have sand in heaven. I hate sand.

"Did you hit your head?"

Did I hit my head? I'm not sure.

Wait. I'm in pain. My knee hurts. My back hurts. It all comes rushing back to me. Watford. The bike. The stairs.

I sit up, and the hem of my dress flops down to cover my Wednesday panties. I bought them because they were silky and didn't show lines through my clothes, but they have the days of the week printed on them. And they are *showing*.

This is *definitely* not heaven. I'm in hell.

"Oh yeah." I jump to my feet, smoothing my dress over my butt. "I'm totally fine. That was pretty funny, huh?"

The guy closest to me has on reflective sunglasses, but they don't disguise the worry on the rest of his face. "That was one of the worst falls I've ever seen." He reaches out to touch my arm, like he wants to support me but stops. "Are you sure you're okay?"

"Yeah! Of course." I smile and wave off his worry, even though tears prickle my eyes. "I've just got to get the bike and . . ." I spin around, realizing Watford's leash is no longer on my arm.

One of the guys is taller than the rest. Like gargantuan tall. Like a foot taller than me and that's saying something. He points to my leg. "You're bleeding."

I look down at a gash that splits my kneecap. "It's just a scratch." A big scratch. Big enough that the blood is already dripping down my leg and under the strap of my shoe. I'll worry about it later when there aren't people staring at me, probably filming this whole thing. "My dog. Did any of you guys see where he went?"

"Yeah," Mirrored Sunglasses says. "He's in the water. With our ball."

"Oh my gosh, I'm so sorry." I limp toward the lake, yelling for Watford.

Two of the guys peel off, leaving me with Sunglasses and Super Tall. They round up the dog pretty quickly. Watford trots back toward me with the remnant of what was once a soccer ball. He drops it at my feet like an offering.

Is it possible to die from embarrassment? And if so, couldn't I have just died from the fall? My face heats to a million degrees. Sweat beads between my shoulder blades and stings the gash on my knee.

"I'm so sorry. I forgot how much he loves soccer balls. My uncle used to play in the UK, and Watford just destroys every ball he sees, and he must have gone crazy when he saw this one and—" And I'm rambling. I can't seem to make it stop. "I can buy you a new one." I reach for my purse, but it's in the sand a few feet behind the bike, and I realize that the other soccer team—of the game I just crashed into—is waiting impatiently.

"I'll just take him and . . ." I thumb toward the walkway. A guy with a shaved head hands me Watford's leash.

Sunglasses jogs along beside me and picks up the bike while I grab my bag. I pull out a twenty from the cash envelope Aunt Emma left for me to use for food while she's out of town, but he shakes his head.

"Please don't concern yourself."

I realize that Sunglasses has an accent to go along with his Greek god good looks. He is probably Greek for real. Or British. I don't know. Maybe I did hit my head. "Are you sure?"

"Yes." He carries the bike up the stairs for me and puts it on the path. "Can you make it home all right? Should I call someone for you?" He frowns at the dog, forehead bunching in concern.

"We'll be fine. Watford is such a good boy." And he usually is, right until he starts licking the blood off my leg. "Knock it off." I push his nose away.

Sunglasses lets out a little chuckle he's probably been trying to hold back this whole time because a girl in a dress flipped over a bike's handlebars and into his soccer game. If it wasn't me, I'd probably laugh too.

"Gabe!" Super Tall yells, pointing to their opponents. The game is starting again, and they're playing without him.

He hesitates, like he's not sure if he should leave me alone.

"You should go." I try to take the bike off his hands. "Thanks for your help."

"I hate to leave if you're injured." He doesn't relinquish his grip on the handlebars.

"Nope. I'm good." *I'm also lying.*

Sunglasses, aka Gabe, gives me a grin. "You *do* know how to ride a bike, right?"

The heat in my face burns all the way up to my ears. "What? Yes! Of course." I make myself laugh like what he's saying is so silly. It comes out too high-pitched, and I clear my throat. "Everyone knows how to ride a bike."

His dark eyebrows pop up above his glasses. "If you say so. Be safe."

Then he's jogging back to his game, checking over his shoulder once to wave goodbye.

Holy crap. Now I actually have to ride the bike home. I hop on, cursing as it pulls at the wound in my knee, but I'm not going to *walk* away. I can ride until I reach the trees, and then I'll get off again where he or any other members of the pantheon can't see me.

"Watford. Heel."

I swear the dog's expression droops, which is pretty impressive considering his face is always droopy.

"No treats for you."

I pedal off again, trying to ignore the blood pooling between my toes.

Honestly, once I get going, it's not so bad. Watford keeps a decent pace, and as long as I don't have to do any tight turns, I'm fine. Nervous and trembling and mortified, but fine.

When I pull up in front of Aunt Emma's high-rise luxury residence hotel, the Belden-Stratford, Doorman Kevin bounds down the stairs. "Miss Maddie? Are you all right?" He takes the bike from me, balancing it against his hip as he bends over to get a closer look at my leg. "Let's get you inside, and we can call your mom."

So she can ruin everything over a skinned knee? Thanks, but no thanks.

"I'm fine, Kevin. Really."

But he bustles me to the front desk and calls one of the bellhops to wheel the bike up to Emma's apartment. He makes me sit in one of the fancy red-and-gold chairs in front of a low marble table and kick my leg up on top. One of the ladies at the front desk— her tag says *JAN*—brings me a little first aid kit with plenty of bandages and big gauze pads. Watford rolls up against her legs, long tongue lolling out. She pats his head absently like she's used to his affections.

Everyone is so kind, but it's salt on this new embarrassment. I should be used to it at this point. I came by the nickname CalaMaddie McPherson honestly. Just like Calamity Jane, accidents like this seek me out. My eyes sting almost as much as my knee. Not only did everyone on Lake Michigan and a group of super-hot guys see my epic crash, but now, everyone in the lobby of this ridiculously expensive hotel knows that something happened too.

I manage to extract myself from Jan and Kevin's care, promising to call my mom as soon as I'm upstairs, and limp to the elevators with Watford trailing behind me. At least I wore him out. He walks straight to his water dish below the floor-to-ceiling windows overlooking Lincoln Park and starts to slurp. I drop onto one of the tufted barstools at the island that divides the kitchen from the living room to take a look at my gash. I've had worse.

Like the scar on my chin from slipping in a puddle of soda at the mall two years ago. Eight stitches that time. I've got a permanent bump on my left forearm from a battle I lost with the stairs at my grandma's house. My mom always says that if a disaster is going to happen, it's going to happen to me. To make me feel better, my older brother, Max, emailed me a study proving that one in twenty-nine people is naturally more accident-prone. It suggested that a lot of those people are risk-takers: never me. Some are multi-taskers, trying to do too many things at once: probably me. Others just have bad luck: totally me.

I reach for my phone because this is the kind of thing that I tell Max. He's great about laughing *with* me or at least helping me see twenty ways the accident could have been worse—his brain runs on probabilities and statistics—but the little flap covering the pocket of my purse is open. My stomach lurches like I've just gone over the handlebars again, and I know without digging through my bag that my phone is gone.

I'm going to have to go back and look for it.

THREE

*I*F I HAVE TO GO BACK TO THE SCENE OF THE INCIDENT TO SCOUR the sand, I'm not doing it in this ridiculous dress. I limp-run to my room, throw on a pair of old cutoffs and a plain black tank.

Watford quirks his head as I put on my flip-flops. "I'll be back soon, you mongrel—"

Wait. What is that noise? I spin around in a circle, tracing the sound. It's definitely a *brrring*. I jog into Aunt Emma's room and there on the bedside table is an *old* phone. The kind they have in hotels, which makes sense since the Belden-Stratford is technically a hotel.

I hesitate before I pick up the beige, corded thing. "Hello?"

"Maddie!"

"Mom?"

She lets out a big, relieved sigh. "This guy called me from the beach, and he said he had your phone, but he sort of had an accent and I thought he said he *had you*. And I asked him, 'Is this some sort of sick joke?' And he said—"

This. This is why I can't go home. "Mom! Relax. Slow down a little bit. Someone has my phone?"

"Yes! And that proves I was *right*. Remember when I made you add me as your emergency contact on your lock screen? Well, it worked. And someone found your phone. He said something about needing to play another soccer game on North Avenue Beach, so he'll be there for a while. I tried to call Emma, but her phone went straight to voice mail. So——"

"Yeah. Emma's in this crazy meeting, and she asked me to take Watford home." Not a lie. None of that was a lie. Emma is headed to a meeting and as far as I know it's crazy. And if I tell my mom that meeting is in another country, she's going to drive straight to Chicago from our hometown of Normal, Illinois. And the last thing I need right now is for her to remind me how completely incapable I am.

"She'll be home later." *Much later.*

"Okay, well. You should wait for her and then——"

"No!" I choke down the panic rising in my chest and pace a few steps away from the nightstand, only to be pulled back by the curly cord. How did people ever use these things? "Mom, it's fine. I don't want to bother her, and the sun is still up, and I've got Watford."

He pokes his head through the bedroom door, ears perked as if I've called for him. Devil Dog. None of this would have happened if not for him.

"But if there are a lot of people, then someone could snatch you."

"Motherrrr. I am seventeen years old." She forgets this fact *constantly.*

She sighs again, and this time, I hear resignation in her voice. "Well." Mom says nothing for a long while, and I can imagine her in our kitchen. Her laptop is probably open on the counter, her newest book on the screen. Although at this stage it's not actually a book; it's just an idea. She's had a lot of *ideas* over the past ten years but hasn't sold any of them to publishers.

"Well," she says again because that's what she says when she's trying to figure her way into the winning side of a conversation, which is all the time.

"I'll be fine." I drop to the side of Aunt Emma's bed, and Watford plunges his face directly into my crotch. This. Darn. Dog.

"Just get there and get back."

I can't help but smile in relief. There's still worry brimming her voice, but it isn't spilling over into an emergency situation. "I'll call you as soon as I have my phone."

She gives me his name—Gabe, of course—and his number in case I can't find him and then says, "I really miss you, Mads."

The sink turns on in the background. She's probably washing dishes while we talk. Mom may freak out once in a while, but she never wastes time. There's probably something in the crockpot and a load of laundry on the couch that I'm not there to fold. I ignore the self-condemnation that rises with that thought. I'm pretty sure that's what she wants me to feel, anyway.

"I miss watching *Star Trek* reruns with the only other Trekkie in the house. And I wish you were here to take your little brother to math camp," she continues, driving the spike of guilt in deeper. I can imagine the pile of worksheets she makes my younger brother do even though school is officially out. "Heaven knows Max doesn't have time to help me."

Gotta give Mom credit for staying on brand. This is so completely expected, that even though today sucked I'm still glad I'm in Chicago, breaking out of the box she keeps me in. Normal was a fine place to grow up for the most part, but it's just small enough and my last name is just uncommon enough to make me the "other" McPherson.

"*Are you Max McPherson's little sister?*" every teacher, administrator, and coach would ask, failing to hide the awe in their voice.

I can't count the number of times I considered lying, but there was no point. Max and I have the same shade of brown hair, the same gray eyes, the same gap between our front teeth until orthodontia gave us matching smiles. We are still confused for twins—he's fourteen months older—but our similarities are only physical.

Max is a certifiable genius. Pretty much everyone in Normal knows his IQ and his GPA, 146 and 4.8, respectively. He's also a great athlete, good member of the community, and a literal Boy Scout. And as such, I've always been a huge disappointment to anyone who knew him first. Max is "gifted." I'm normal.

I'd probably hate him if he wasn't also one of the nicest humans in existence.

On bad days, I hate him a little anyways.

There *are* negative side effects to living your entire life in your older brother's shadow. People (read: parents) start to believe you belong there.

I hold in a sigh. I know I mean more to Mom than a dishwasher, laundry folder, and a younger sibling chauffeur. She and Dad say they want the "best" for me, but sometimes it just feels like they want what's safe and easy. With Max, they push him to reach for his dreams, expect him to apply and get premier scholarships, but when I told them about my dream school and program they both responded with something like, "Wouldn't it be better to pursue something you're good at?" and "Stick with what you can achieve, Maddie." That's why I've gotta make it happen on my own.

"I love you, Mom."

"Call me as soon as you have it."

"I will. Promise."

I clip Watford's leash back on his harness—I can at least be honest in that part—and we rush out of the building. Kevin is singing some gospel song as he waits under the awning, and his voice is a gorgeous, rich baritone. He stops the minute I push through the rotating door, concern showing under his flat-brimmed uniform hat. "Where you headed, Miss Maddie?"

It wouldn't surprise me if Emma asked him to keep an eye on me. She's subtler than my mom, but still a worrier underneath. "Just back to the beach. I dropped my phone."

"You sure you don't want me to call a cab?"

My leg hurts, but it's not that bad. Plus, waiting for a cab might take as long as it would to walk down there. "No, but thank you."

He goes back to humming the same song, but I can feel his eyes on me as I hurry away.

I take the most direct path, cutting across the park to get to the beach faster, not even reveling in the gorgeous flower beds. Watford trots along beside me, getting pulled up short every time he stops to sniff the trees or fire hydrants. I'm not putting up with any more of his crap.

As the grandstand comes into view, I worry that maybe I won't recognize this Gabe guy. Besides the reflective glasses and godlike body, I don't really remember what he looks like. Luckily, I don't have to search long. He's leaning against the side of the bleachers, Super Tall and a group of guys beside him, laughing about something. Probably me.

Super Tall notices me—or Watford first—and raises his chin in my direction.

Suddenly, nervousness bites. Little prickles creep over my skin as Gabe peels himself off the side of the grandstand and moves toward me, a smile on his face.

"Hi," I say, as he gets closer. "Thanks for finding my phone and calling my mom."

Watford lunges toward him, but Gabe drops to a knee beside the dog, ruffling his ears. "Of course. How's your leg?"

I look down at the gauze patch Jan taped over the gash on my knee, face flaming in embarrassment. "It's fine. Nothing a Band-Aid couldn't fix."

He straightens and pushes his sunglasses on top of his head, revealing hazel eyes rimmed with thick black lashes. Something about his face pings in my memory. Where have I seen him before?

In your dreams.

Okay, fine. He's gorgeous. If you see a face like that in person, you don't forget where.

"I'm glad you're all right. And your name is Maddie?"

Why does he care? Do I care if he cares? I mean—I take a closer look—he's not that much older than me. Maybe eighteen? Nineteen? Suddenly, I do care that he wants to know my name. "Yes. Maddie. Madeline McPherson."

Belatedly, I hold out my hand. The grin on his face goes a little crooked, but he shakes it, hanging on for a second longer than necessary. Either the sun went supernova or I'm blushing. The back of my ears are on fire.

"And this is Watford? Such an unusual name."

I lick my lips. I should flirt, right? Or at least try not to act like I'm suffering from a concussion. "Yeah. He's my aunt's dog. I'm just watching him for the weekend. My uncle—well, my former uncle—named him. I guess he didn't like the soccer team from that city, so he thought it was hysterical to name an ugly dog after them."

Gabe laughs, then looks over his shoulder to where his friends are waiting. They're not watching us, but I can still feel them checking us out every now and then. "Your uncle likes Premier League football?"

He says football like "*futbol*," and I remember that he's probably European. Max could probably identify Gabe's country of origin from his accent and then converse fluently in his native tongue. "Not *liked*," I say. "He played for a long time. For Arsenal, I think?"

I don't think. I *know*. Before he became The Cheating Bastard, we all had jerseys with his name on the back. I used to love to watch his games. It's where my obsession with sports business really started.

Gabe's eyebrows pop up, surprised. It's sort of nice that I can use my ex-uncle's career for some benefit. Considering what he did to Aunt Emma, something good should come out of my association with him.

"What's his name?"

I almost refer to him as The Cheating Bastard because that's all any of us have called him for the last four years. His affair with an American Olympian was splashed all over the tabloids in the UK, coinciding with his retirement from professional soccer. My blush flashes to anger on Aunt Emma's behalf. She covered for him, saving his career and all his sponsorships, playing the forgiving wife. Then, once it was out of the news, she quietly divorced him, took half of everything he owned—and his dog. She did it with such savvy and tact that Velocity Marketing hired her to help their problem clientele.

"You probably wouldn't recognize it," I say, trying to tug Watford back toward me, but he isn't having any of that. "He's been out of the league for a few years."

Gabe gives me an expectant look and I wish I hadn't said anything besides, *Phone. Now.*

Finally, I mumble, "Geoffrey Jones."

There's a long pause as Gabe evaluates this information. I can feel
his disbelief like a slap to the face. "Your uncle is Geoffrey Jones?"

I nod, not blaming him for the doubt. "Can I have my phone,
please?"

"Wait." The funniest expression crosses his face, like he's tasted
something bitter and wants to spit it out. "Your uncle is the greatest
midfielder of all time?"

"*Ex*-uncle." There's no way he can miss the emphasis on The
Cheating Bastard's unofficial title. "And as far as the greatest what-
ever, I wouldn't know. I don't really do the whole soccer fan thing."
Anymore.

He hesitates, then swings the sack-style backpack off his shoulder, digs around, and hands me my phone, miraculously no worse
for wear.

"No offense, but your uncle is an . . ." He pauses, as if looking
for the right term. "Asshat?"

"Yes." I smile, relieved that he doesn't worship at the Geoffrey
Jones altar like most of the soccer-loving world. "Or Bastard."

"Bastardo." He nods like we've come to an agreement on
something.

We both laugh and a little attraction zings around my belly. "Well.
Thank you." Gah! I sound like my mother instead of Aunt Emma.
"Can I buy you a bottle of Gatorade or a hot dog or something?"

As soon as it's out of my mouth, I wish I could take it back. "Out
of gratitude, I mean."

"I'm actually headed out with my friends." He checks over his
shoulder at the group of people who are looking a little irritated

that he's taking so long. "Would you like to come with us?"

Yes. "Oh. I can't." And by that, I mean I shouldn't. Leaving with four guys, some of whom are clearly *much* older than I am, is a pretty dumb idea. Even for someone with a normal IQ. "I really should get Watford home."

The dog is lying across Gabe's feet. I know Aunt Emma walks him a lot, so he's probably not tired, but it's a good enough excuse.

Gabe buys it. "Do you bring him to the beach a lot?"

"Yes." Of course not. I haven't brought him anywhere until today, but because Gabe is ridiculously hot and talking to me with something that feels like interest, I lie. "And to the dog park."

"Maybe I'll see you here sometime?" He cocks one eyebrow, and I wonder if he's practiced that expression in the mirror or if he comes by this charm and gloriousness naturally.

I tilt my head, aiming for coy but probably missing. "Maybe you will."

He walks off, looking back over his shoulder and waving once, just like he did after he helped me get on the bike.

I nibble my bottom lip and return his wave, praying that I'll bump—without actual physical bumping—into him again.

Four

I SPEND THE ENTIRE WEEKEND NURSING MY WOUNDS, DEBATING whether or not to text Gabe (I decide against it), and watching all of the TV shows that are forbidden at home. Weirdly exhausted and bruised, I startle out of my Advil PM–induced coma at six on Monday morning. Watford is standing over me, breathing loudly, instead of hogging the whole bed and shoving his giant paws against my back.

He gives a soft *woof* of warning.

"What is it, Watty?" I whisper. It's not that I expect him to answer, but I swear he understands the tone of my voice. "Did you hear something?"

He doesn't move, and a strand of drool stretches closer to my nose, so I push him away as I try to figure out what woke us up.

My cell phone screen is glowing, meaning it must have been ringing. I've got a missed call from Aunt Em. She's supposed to be in London until tomorrow. My heart races to an even higher rate. I can't imagine her calling me this early without it being an emergency.

She picks up on the first ring. "Thank goodness. No one is answering their phones." There's beeping and shuffling in the background.

"Em?"

"Yes. Sorry. I'm just leaving O'Hare. I know it's early, but you'd think one of my employees would be awake by now. I've already sent an email, but I need to make sure that it's handled immediately."

I legitimately have no idea what she's talking about. "What email? What's handled?"

"We've got a client issue, and I need someone to pick up a breakfast catering order."

She's calling about a catering order? At six o'clock in the morning? "Okay."

My aunt knows me well enough to hear the question in my voice. "I've got Scott Van Baxter coming in at seven for a planning meeting. He's got a problem client who made a mess this weekend, and I'm working on a plan to turn that around. It'll be tight to get there from the airport, but I need to make sure breakfast is set up in the Lakeside conference room."

I've only been interning for like five minutes, but everyone knows Scott Van Baxter is the biggest agent in the business. Working with him is a huge deal, so I understand Emma's concern.

"I'll take care of it."

"Thanks, Mads. I knew I could count on you." There's a smile in her voice. "The order will be in my name at Allium, the restaurant on the Delaware side of the building."

"Got it."

"See you in an hour."

I'm already moving before I hang up. I need to prove Aunt Emma right about the internship and so much more. Last Thanksgiving, I heard her whisper-arguing with my mom about me trying to get into the University of North Carolina. She was pissed that my parents didn't want me to apply to her alma mater and wanted an explanation. My mom said UNC was suited for people who were naturally good at school, not people who study for three hours every night to get good grades in high school. Emma told her that I had grit and determination and they should support me. Then Cube walked in and I'm not sure how the conversation ended, but since then Aunt Em has been on Team Maddie—convincing my parents to let me intern for her company, sneaking me money for extra ACT prep courses.

I want her to know I'm worth that investment. I can be responsible and helpful and not a walking disaster.

On the bus to work, I text my brother Max and give him the breakdown of my weekend, including the crash. He sends me every laughing emoji, some GIFs of people walking into walls, and a link to a song called "Dumb Ways to Die." If it had been anyone else, I'd probably be pissed, but Max doesn't pity me. He laughs, and he's loyal. He's exactly the brother I need.

My heart pinches, and I realize (not for the first time) that I'm really going to miss him next year.

I make it to the restaurant just before seven, but it takes the waiter five minutes to find Emma's order and five more to show me every box of breakfast goods. I know this is part of his job and that I shouldn't be frustrated, but there's a clock in my head that's ticking louder with every second that passes. Is Emma back already? Are the clients already there?

The walk back to the office takes too long. The elevator moves too slow. And when it opens onto Velocity's lobby, the front desk is unmanned. The giant white catering bags cut into my arms as I rush toward the conference room. Leaning close to the smoked glass door, I hear the low buzz of voices.

I'm late.

I lever the handle down slowly, turn to the side, and slide

through the narrow door frame. From the corner of my eye, I see Aunt Em sitting on the window side of the table—the blinds have been lowered and closed tight—and across from her is a man who looks like he might play linebacker for the Bears. Partially hidden by his bulk is another body, slumped in the chair, arms folded, hoodie pulled up.

Problem client for sure.

Magazines and newspapers litter the table between them (probably more tabloids I'll have to comb through later) and a slim charcoal folder with the Velocity logo is open in front of Em.

"The simplest way to solve this problem is for him to lie low for the next month, stay focused on his on-field play, and be advised—"

"This ain't his first offense," the agent interrupts with a surprisingly heavy Southern accent. "Heck, this isn't his *fifth* offense. He can't just lie low and hope people forget. We've gotta turn this around. Management isn't happy. Sponsors aren't interested. We need a Hail Mary. If we don't get this worked out, I don't know that anyone in the whole flippin' world is gonna want him either."

"Oh please," says a disgruntled, gravelly voice. "Someone will want me. I can go to Eredivisie if I have to."

I pretend not to listen as I set the first bag on the floor next to my feet and the second on the top of the sideboard. There's way too much food for this little space.

"That's not the point," the agent says. "You're too valuable for some backwater Dutch city. You're worth too much for MLS."

"It all comes back to your cut of my paycheck, doesn't it?"

Cringing a little at the venom in the client's voice, I slide the water jug and a stack of Velocity-branded plastic cups to the side so I can make more room for the coffee and pastries.

"You signed with me 'cause you knew I was the best. 'Cause

you wanted the best!" A fist thumps against the table. I jump at the noise, and my elbow bumps the cups, sending them cascading off the edge and clinking into the metal blinds with more noise than I could have imagined possible.

I peek over my shoulder, hoping that my little disaster has gone unnoticed.

It hasn't. All three heads have turned toward me.

"Sorry," I whisper, but I freeze before I reach for the cups.

Em's face is blank. The agent's face is red. But it's the third face—with dark, slightly curly hair peeking out from the edge of his hoodie, lips parted in surprise, and hazel eyes rimmed with thick black lashes—that has me stuck in a demi-plié.

The problem client is the guy from the beach. The problem client is . . . Gabe.

I don't know how long I stand like that, but it's long enough that Em says my name and nods at me to get moving.

"Sorry," I say again, even softer this time, and start cleaning up my mess.

A chair rolls out from the table, and I feel a presence behind me. Gabe is holding out one of the cups that must have rolled away.

"Is this some sort of a joke?" he asks, looking from me to the table and back. His face is hard, the sardonic grin doing nothing for his good looks. "A setup?"

"What?" Confusion lines Em's forehead. "This is our newest intern—"

"Madeline McPherson," Gabe finishes for her, and gives a cold laugh. "We met on the beach this weekend. Wasn't that . . . fortuitous?"

Fortuitous isn't exactly the word I would have used. *Catastrophic. Cataclysmic. Awful.*

"Scott, do you have someone spying on me?" Gabe gestures to Emma with the cup. "I've been stalked by paparazzi. I've had women sneak into my hotel rooms. But this . . ." He finishes with a shake of his head.

I pick up the food boxes, trying to move as quickly and quietly as I can. I have to get out of this room. Like now.

"What are you talking about?" Scott says, sounding perplexed enough that I don't need to look at him to imagine the expression on his face.

"The bike crash. The dog." Gabe's words are directed at my back. "Were you hoping that I'd rescue you and then . . . what exactly?"

"It was just an accident," I say, staying focused on the boxes. "I had—have—no idea who you are."

"I'm Gabriel Fortunato. *Everyone* knows who I am."

Gabriel Fortunato. I've heard that name. Soccer. MLS. The pieces are starting to line up. I turn slowly to face my aunt, the agent, and Gabe. And then it all clicks. Gabriel Fortunato. The Italian soccer player who missed the goal in last year's World Cup shoot-out and wrapped his Maserati around a telephone pole shortly after.

"The bike crash was a little over the top." Gabe holds out the cup to me, lowering his voice to a stage whisper. "But the Wednesday panties certainly got my attention."

"What in God's holy name is going on here, Emma?" Scott thumps the table again.

Emma's face is pale, her mango-colored lipstick a bright slash against her pallor. "I'd like an explanation myself."

I can't get enough air in my lungs. Black spots blot across my vision.

Gabe must see my panic because his face softens. He pushes back his hood. "*Oddio*. It *was* an accident?"

I take a deep breath in through my nose and blow it out through my mouth, trying to find some sort of center. "Em, remember how I rode your bike home on Friday? Well, I was a little out of practice, and I had Watford, and when he saw the sand soccer tournament and the ball bounced toward us—you know how he gets around soccer balls, so—"

Gabe flinches like he just took a hard kick to the shins.

"So Watford dove down the steps and pulled the bike with him and I crashed and . . ." I pause to pull up the hem of my skirt to show the bandage on my knee as if the evidence will save me. "And Gabe—or Gabriel, is it Gabriel?—stopped in the middle of his game—"

"Wait." Scott's voice stops the flow of my verbal diarrhea. He points at Gabriel. "You were *playing* in the sand soccer tournament?"

"I wasn't alone. It was just for fun." Suddenly, Gabe is defending himself in his native language, and shockingly, his agent is responding in Italian, although it's slathered with a biscuits and gravy drawl. At least for the moment, I'm out of the hot seat.

Emma catches my eye across the room and mouths, "Run while you can."

And I do.

ONE OF THE INTERNS THAT I MET BRIEFLY ON FRIDAY, MARA, IS sitting at the front desk. She looks up as I rush past her, but I pretend not to see her raised eyebrows and half-open mouth as I swing open the secret door.

I whip past William's office and collapse into my cubicle chair. Elbows on desk. Head in hands. Questions ping around my brain like pinballs in the old arcade pizza place our family used to go to on Saturdays. What just happened? *Ping*. Gabriel Fortunato?!? *Beep-boop*. How could I possibly be so stupid? *Pong*. Also, what did he do to get into so much trouble since Friday? *Brrrp. Game. Over.*

Aunt Emma told me to run, but my gut—and the last growly words from his agent—says that Gabe has dug himself a ditch too deep to climb out without help.

My fingers fly over my keyboard as I log into Velocity's creepy, stalkerish news-combing program and search his name. The nastiest gossip sites play a video of a glassy-eyed Gabe stumbling out of a club late Saturday night with his arm around the shoulders of a girl in a short, sparkly dress that shows off her killer legs.

The words *drunken brawl* and *contract violation* scroll across my screen. I plug my earbuds into the laptop to hear the voice-over.

"The Italian stallion's management has been hush-hush about what actually happened in Mexico, but according to witnesses, MLS pretty boy Gabriel Fortunato escalated an argument to a shoving match, taking a punch to the chin. Ouch! Important side note for those not in the know: American laws prohibit nineteen-year-olds from hitting the clubs and boozing it up, so it looks like he spent some of his millions to charter a flight to a country where the laws are a little more lax. Not that silly things like laws have stopped this soccer hotshot in the past."

The footage cuts to a still photo of a bright red sports car—or at least what's left of it. A telephone pole rests against what would have been the passenger seat. The roof is partially caved in, and the windshield is opaque with fractures. I stifle a gasp. How in the world did he survive that? How could anyone survive that?

The gossip reporter continues:

"The boozy brawl comes on the heels of last summer's—yikes—car wreck after Italy's failed attempt at taking the World Cup title. While Fortunato wasn't charged with driving under the influence, he was slapped on the wrist with a ticket for excessive speed and reckless driving."

The next shot is of Gabe, shirt off, sunglasses on, smiling smugly at the camera while two women in bikinis drape themselves across him. Gag. What makes it worse is that it's so posed and airbrushed and perfect that it looks like an advertisement. The voice-over fades to a buzz in the background as I lean a little closer to the screen, eyes squinted to see where Photoshop has done its magic.

"Trust me. The real thing is better," a voice behind me says.

I bolt to my feet, forgetting the earbuds still attached to the laptop, which jerks off the edge of the desk. I manage to catch it before it plummets to a fiery death. My desk chair rolls backward into the open doorway. There Gabe stands in his hoodie-clad glory, gripping the chair's high back and wearing an expression I can't quite name. Confused amusement, maybe?

"Getting caught looking at naughty pictures is a little embarrassing," he says, head canting to the side with all sorts of arrogant condemnation.

"It's more embarrassing to pose for them," I shoot back. Fold arms across chest, lean hip against desk, cross ankles. Assume self-congratulatory expression.

His eyes widen in momentary surprise, but then that cocky grin spreads across his face like he knows I'm acting.

Be cool. I'm so cool. I got this.

"Look, what happened on Friday was totally an accident." My throat burns with humiliation, but I manage to choke out the rest of the words. "Sorry I crashed into your game. I had no idea who you were, and I honestly don't care."

Okay, that didn't come out *quite* the way I meant it.

"I know it was an accident. Even my most desperate fans haven't gone that far yet." A little laugh flavors his words. "And Emma— she's your aunt, yes?—said that Watford is a very difficult animal sometimes."

"Great. Thanks for clearing that up." Literally no gratitude in my voice. Now what? Why is he here? How did he find me?

Wednesday panties, my brain so helpfully supplies. *He remembered they said Wednesday.*

"Wait." I look over my right shoulder toward the hidden door. "How *did* you find my cubicle?"

Gabe leans back a little and gives a chin tilt to someone at the end of the row. And I realize that we have an audience. Because this day just keeps getting better. Mara gives him a timid wave, while the other two repeat interns—Javi and Arman—watch with undisguised glee. Katie looks like she's going to burst because a tabloid-worthy scene is happening in our office. Where are the actual paparazzi when all the best stuff is going down?

Mortification battles anger, and both emotions push me into action. I grab a random stack of paper off my desk. "Could you please move? I need to make some copies."

Confusion wrinkles the space between Gabe's eyebrows. He doesn't budge. "Okay . . ." He stuffs his hands in the front pocket of his hoodie. His focus drops to the patterned carpet between his feet. "I actually came to apologize."

"For what?"

He looks up at me through his eyelashes—an expression I'm sure he's cultivated because he looks deceptively innocent. "I know what it's like to be accused of something you didn't do. And I'm sorry I called you a stalker."

"You didn't."

He gives a full-bodied shrug and sheepish grin. "I thought it."

How am I supposed to respond to that? "Gee, thanks"? He must see the lack of acceptance on my face because the little dimples that bracket his mouth disappear. "I'm sorry if I caused you any embarrassment. That's all."

"Oh." I square the papers in my hand, ignoring the way my sweaty palms stick to them. "Well, thank you."

He signals for me to exit in front of him, and I do because, even though I don't actually have anywhere to go, I'm not going to admit that now. The other interns have disappeared back into their cubicles, and William's still shut in his office. Thank heavens.

When I open the hidden door, Gabe catches and holds it like he's some sort of gentleman in an old movie. It also means he's right behind me. I murmur a quiet thanks over my shoulder and my eyes snag on his for a second. I almost trip as I step into the lobby.

Then, I realize who's standing at the front desk and stop so fast that Gabe steps on the back of my shoe. His hand is at my waist. Steadying me or him? I'm not sure with his chest against my shoulder blades.

Emma is leaning one forearm against the high front desk, face a thunderstorm as she listens to whatever Scott is hissing. The agent stops midsentence, and both heads swing our way.

Scott takes a breath, then he lets it out without saying whatever thought was on his tongue. "I didn't think you would still be here." His words are soft, and his lips are pressed thin.

"I'm on my way out." Gabe's hand drops from my side, or maybe it was already gone and I just now noticed.

"With Maddie?" Emma manages to ask without any condemnation or concern in her tone, but there's something brewing behind her eyes. She and my mom might have completely different personalities, but they share the same expressions, and this one is dangerous.

"No. I was getting copies." I look down at the papers in my hands—it's a pamphlet for in-office pedicures with a picture of nasty, fungus-encrusted toenails on the front. Even better. "Unless you need something? Can I get you anything? Any of you? Emma? Mr. . . ." Oh my gosh I can't remember his name. It's totally floated out of my mind with the words spilling over my lips. "Scott?"

"Actually . . ." Emma's eyes are narrow, flitting from me to Gabe and back. "Why don't you follow me back to the conference room. Both of you."

EMMA LEANS BACK IN HER CHAIR, ELBOWS RESTING ON THE WIDE armrests, stilettoed foot bouncing under the table. She's wearing her poker face. It's probably unreadable to other people, but I've spent the last five years playing Texas Hold'em with her after every holiday dinner. We had to relegate Max to dealer because he counts cards. My dad is a half-decent player and we've lost some big penny pots to him, but more often than not, I've ended up playing heads-up against Em. She's not afraid to take a risk if the payoff is good enough, and I swear I can see her mentally tallying her chips.

Scott has switched sides of the table, sitting directly across from Gabriel Fortunato. Something about the positioning makes me think that they're presenting a united front. Team Emma/Scott is about to face off against Team Maddie/Gabe. I'm not sure how I've ended up on a team with Gabe, and I'm not certain that I like it. There's no way he can be oblivious to the tension in the room—considering I can actually hear the seams in Scott's suit straining against his frustration—but Gabe's staring down into what must now be a lukewarm cup of coffee like he'll find his future in its dregs.

"Gabe, you've made it abundantly clear that you hate social media and don't like to be coached, overseen, and . . ." Emma pauses, flipping closed the folder that's in front of her with a snap. "What was it you said?"

He looks up from his drink. "Minded."

"Right." Emma pushes the folder across the table to me. "Would you be more amenable to participating in our efforts if say . . . Maddie . . . was your contact for this campaign?"

"What?" Gabe asks, and Scott and I both echo.

Emma holds up a manicured hand, stopping everyone before we can utter any complaints. "Give me a second to explain. The first phase of Reputation Recovery is to create a positive social media presence. I've laid out a plan." She nods to the folder.

I open the cover and look over the strategies my aunt has made to improve his public persona, which include a content calendar with video and photo ideas, suggested text for social media posts, and goodwill events he'll be expected to attend. The first four weeks are laid out around his practice and game schedules, while the next few months are described in broader terms.

Talk about building a brand. Emma's got Gabe's image pinned down like he's one of the character sketches my mom does for her romance novels. In Emma's version, he's a regular guy doing a great job balancing talent, fame, and his personal life. She's given him a very specific voice—pleasant and friendly—and a consistent feel, down to suggested filters to use on his Instagram feed.

"This is amazing, Em."

She shrugs off my compliment. "It's great in theory, but Gabe has to buy in to make it work."

He grumbles and slumps deeper into his chair. Scott's face turns red, but he doesn't call his client to heel.

"I want it to feel more organic, more natural, and we really want to hit that eighteen to twenty-five demographic. If we let the two of you—who are representative of our target market—direct the content, then I think we may stand a better chance of achieving our goals." She pats Scott on the arm reassuringly. "Nothing will post without my or William's approval, but we'll let you two handle *some* of the development."

I don't mention that I'm not technically in the age bracket—

I won't be eighteen until November—because there's a little bubble of excitement sitting at the back of my throat. Katie said that interns have to jump on opportunities to prove themselves, and I don't think I'm going to get anything better than this.

Em gives me a little smile. "I think you could be a good team. Maddie's trying to get into a prestigious sports marketing program, so I *know* she'll only bring her best work to the table. And Gabe doesn't want to stay in MLS, so they both have reasons to deliver."

I can see Scott turning all of this over in his head, giant arms folded across his chest, chin stuck out. He doesn't like it, but for some reason he's considering it. Is it because he trusts Emma's judgment or because he's willing to try anything to get Gabe under control?

"We've got about two weeks left in MLS's break for the Gold Cup. We'll use the first week to create content with a launch scheduled for next Monday," Emma continues. "When the season starts back up, we'll reevaluate or change direction as needed."

Two weeks doesn't give me time to either make an impression or screw anything up too badly. Scott must be thinking the same thing because he relaxes his shoulders and his suit jacket sighs in relief.

Gabe rests his elbows on the table, cup settled between his palms. The ring finger on his right hand taps against its side as he mulls it over. "All right."

His agreement obliterates my excitement, and the remnants sink to the bottom of my stomach. My brain runs through a hundred ways this could go wrong, but before I can voice any of my fears, Scott speaks.

"This better work, Emma. If it doesn't, I'm out and I'm taking all my clients with me." He pushes back from the chair and stands. "You're not getting any more chances, Gabe. Don't screw this up."

And with that ultimatum he leaves.

Em reacts as if Scott's departure is no big deal. "Tomorrow we'll get some footage of Gabe training with his team to start off our social media blast, then the two of you can get together later this week to hash out some ideas." She passes a blank notepad across the table to Gabe. "Gabriel, we'll need you to change your social media passwords to something we can access, and then I'll walk you out."

He takes the pad and scribbles two quick lines before standing up to follow Emma to the lobby. "See you tomorrow, I guess."

Gabe gives me this sort of shy half-smile, and I'm reminded that he's the kind of gorgeous that makes it hard to breathe.

As they walk out, I pull the paper toward me. The first line is his phone number, and the second says, "All passwords will be changed to WEDNESDAY7."

Just kidding. Gabriel Fortunato is hideous.

Six

ARA'S STILL AT THE FRONT DESK WHEN I LEAVE THE CONFER-
ence room, but now Katie has joined her. I can practically
see questions brimming on their lips.

"How come you guys are at the front desk?" I ask, hoping to
change directions before they can drag me down the trail of what
just happened. "Is Patty out sick or something?"

"She's on vacation for the week, so all of us interns will take
turns filling in," Katie says, handing me a calendar handwritten
in bright pink. "Sorry, I probably should have mentioned that on
Friday. We've got a schedule worked out, so that no one is stuck
here all day."

Two things stand out to me immediately: Katie and I are slotted
for twice as many hours as the other three interns, which I guess
makes sense, since we're considered "general office interns" instead
of being assigned to one of the senior executives. But I'm also
scheduled to be on the desk for most of Tuesday.

"Is there any way I can switch with someone? Something has
come up for tomorrow."

Mara leans forward, eyes narrow. "Does that *something* have to
do with Gabriel Fortunato?"

"Girl, I'm so glad you asked." Katie grabs Mara's upper arm. "I have no idea who he is, but I've been dying—*dying*!—since he walked in. The accent. The cheekbones. Full swoon."

Besides a quick hello on Friday, I haven't had any interaction with Mara. Everything I know about her came from one of Katie's rumor-filled monologues. Apparently, Mara just finished her junior year at USC, really does have ridiculously shiny hair, spends her free time doing Brazilian jiujitsu, and she and William sort of had a thing last year. It fizzled out when he stayed at Velocity to start his career and she went back to school. Katie thinks there's still some friction there and is waiting for something juicy to happen.

Both girls watch me like vultures, expecting a delicious bit of gossip to be dropped in front of them.

"I don't really know him. I just . . . ran into him this one time on the beach." *Nicely understated, Mads.* "We talked for a few minutes, but I had no idea who he was—still don't, really—but we *know of* each other."

"And that was enough to prompt him to find your cubicle?" Mara asks, face disbelieving. "Because he seemed a little . . ."

"Flirty," Katie so helpfully supplies.

"Oh no. Definitely not. He's a client and it looks like I'll be helping my aunt on his account a little bit just because we've already met and *know of* each other." I literally could not sound more ridiculous. Just. Stop. Talking.

Mara's posture straightens, her hands dropping to the desktop. "You're going to be working on the Fortunato account?"

There is ice in her tone, and from the worried, wide-eyed expression on Katie's face, she hears it too.

"Yeah. Just helping with some social media stuff. It's totally no big deal." I smile and wave it off.

"Isn't this your *second* day?"

I look to Katie for help, but she's shaking her head subtly.

"Ummm . . . yes?"

"This is so typical." Mara stands up with a huff. "Since you're going to be so busy with the Fortunato account tomorrow, you can take my shift *now*."

She bolts for the secret door, leaving me and Katie staring at each other across the receptionist desk.

"For some reason," Katie says, as she turns to watch the door shut, "I get the sense that Mara's a little unhappy."

It's such an understatement that I laugh. "What am I supposed to do? Tell her that I'm sorry? Offer to trade with her?"

"No! Also, why would you? Gabriel Fortunato—who I'm Googling right now—just fell into your lap. You take that . . ." Her voice fades as images load on her phone.

"Katie?" I lean across the top of the desk to see what she's looking at. Link after link of headlines like "Hot Mess Soccer Star" and "Chicago Fire Star Comes Under Fire . . . Again" fill her screen.

She looks up at me and scrunches her nose. "At least he's nice to look at."

KATIE GIVES ME A THIRTY-SECOND CRASH COURSE ON HOW TO ACCEPT and transfer calls and shows me how to log in to Patty's computer so I can get my interoffice email before she goes back to collating copies for William. Chaos ensues. Phones are ringing. The elevator is pinging. And I have sweat dripping down to my elbows.

Okay, not literal sweat. But it feels like I should be sweating.

I disconnect the first two people I try to transfer—I know because they call back and yell at me—and maybe a third one, before I finally get the hang of things. Then, the phones stop but the computer dings. There's an email from my aunt that says simply, "Please review" and has an attached file titled "Gabriel Fortunato— PRIVATE."

Besides managing the front desk, I've got one little project to finish for William before I can dig into Gabriel Fortunato's dirt. And I'm actually grateful. Something about the file makes me feel like Aunt Em handed me the key to Gabe's house and told me to rifle through his underwear drawer. When I'm searching through tabloids for other athletes, it's like a history project. I wouldn't worry about the filthy secrets I'd discover about Babe Ruth or Pelé because they aren't anyone I'd meet in real life. They're *figures*, not people.

Gabe is different. He's a boy I spent a weekend daydreaming about, which is ridiculous now that I know who he is. But even so, he was *so* nice to me at the beach both after I crashed and when he returned my phone. He played with Watford. He had a conversation, albeit an uncomfortable one, with my mother. And even after the Wednesday panties comment, he did sort of apologize. I want to hang on to those few shining moments of humanity before I let the tabloids throw shadows.

I take my time collating the presentation William prepared for a ticket-pricing study, hole punch each of the copies, and put them into folders I find in the copy room.

William's office door is shut, but as I raise my fist to knock, it flies open. Mara brushes past me without even making eye contact. Her steps are a little louder than they should be against the carpeted floor.

Still unhappy.

I tap on the door frame before poking my head into William's office. "Hey," I say when he looks up. "Is Mara okay?"

"Yeah. She's fine. Those my copies?" He changes the subject smoothly.

"Yeah. They looked important, so I thought I'd dress them up a bit."

He turns back the cover and flips through the pages. "Nice. I like your attention to detail."

Was that a compliment? Before long he'll call me by my real name. I mentally do a little happy dance. "Thanks—"

"Which is good since I hear you'll be working on the Fortunato account?" His pitch lilts up at the end of the sentence, turning it into a question.

"Yeah. It was a surprise to me too."

"Hmm." He nods a few times, the wheels turning behind his eyes. "Emma's running point, but with her other clients she doesn't have time to helicopter you on this. Everything you intend to post will need my approval before it goes live."

Oh. I sort of thought that I'd be handling the social media on my own. Which is ridiculous because I'm just an intern. Interns don't handle accounts; they make copies and do grunt work.

"Put Emma's plan into play, and don't deviate from the script unless there's a way to upgrade her suggestions. Which you should definitely want to do." He gives me a significant nod.

I envision a little kitten pouncing on a ball of yarn. *No!* my imagination shouts. *You are a lioness. POUNCE!*

"In the end, I'm still responsible for making sure that everything is disseminated, filtered, proofread, and on-brand."

Did he just use the word *disseminated* in a sentence? And actually mean it? "Of course. And Emma wants Gabe to have more involvement in what is posted on his accounts, so I'd planned to get his input." Which is a lie. I hadn't planned anything, but I'm planning it now because I'm a lioness.

William waves off that idea. "I know guys like him. He'll do what we want as long as it doesn't require too much effort on his part. Don't expect Gabe to come up with anything *helpful*." William moves the stack of folders to the corner of his desk, and I get the sense that this conversation is over. Not that I said much.

Feeling like an ignored house cat, I stand, preempting my dismissal. "Is there anything you want me to work on right now?"

"You can look through other players' Instagram feeds to get an idea of what types of things we should post on Gabe's accounts. Emma asked me to be on-site with you tomorrow to help get footage."

"Are we meeting here first?"

He hesitates before answering, and I almost think he's going to tell me not to bother showing up at all. "Be at the stadium by nine a.m. Go straight there. No point commuting twice. How much experience do you have editing video?"

Besides adding hashtags and text? None. "A little."

"I can ask Mara or Arman to help you with Final Cut—"

"No!" I say too loudly, then soften it with a smile. "Thank you, but I can handle it on my own. I'm pretty good at figuring out these sorts of things."

I have no idea what I'm talking about. I don't even know what these *things* are, but I have to impress William. He's the intern manager. He's going to write my letter of recommendation.

"Emma sent me some info. I'll go catch up on everything Fortunato-related and look at the editing program." I'm assuming it's a program. Or an app? Either way, William doesn't stop me as I back out of his office. "See you later. Thanks. Bye."

My ridiculous exit is the least of my worries. What have I gotten myself into?

Seven

Full name: Gabriel Dominic Fortunato

Age: 19

Place of birth: Sanremo, Liguria, Imperia, Italy

Height: 1.89 m (6 feet 2 inches)

Weight: 77.1 kg (170 lb)

Playing position: Forward

Current team: Chicago Fire Soccer Club

Number: 7

THE FIRST PAGE OF GABRIEL'S INFORMATION SHEET READS LIKE a Wikipedia page, including all his career highlights, trophies won, goals scored. It looks like he started to make a name for himself when he was fifteen, which was right around the time I quit watching soccer permanently. That makes me feel a little better about having no clue of his identity.

I skip over his ridiculous list of awards, international appearances, and style of play, and stop after the "Personal Life" section, totally disappointed.

I've attended—or stolen snacks from—enough of my mom's

romance writers' group meetings to know the importance of a good backstory. That tattooed, motorcycle-riding, brooding alpha male secretly has a heart of gold. He rescues puppies or has military scars or a family death he can't forgive himself for. I was hoping I'd find something in Gabe's past that made him redeemable—not that I'm wishing someone murdered his imaginary brother—but it's just not there.

No diseases overcome, no financial hardships, no broken family. It looks like the only excuse for his behavior is privilege, money, and overindulgent parents. From the photograph pasted into the file, his family is the picture of perfect. His dad owns a successful ship-building business and his mom comes from a floriculture dynasty. Which is apparently a thing? There's even a pixelated photo of a much younger Gabe standing with his mom, dad, and a sister in front of a gorgeous field of cultured flowers with an ancient-looking mansion in the background.

When sifting through his past doesn't yield any positive results, I move forward. Onto controversies. Yikes. Red cards. Flagrant fouls. Game suspensions. Words and phrases like *hothead, out of control, fiery temper* are listed in bold, and that's all *before* the car wreck. Some people believed he was drunk, others said it was a suicide attempt. For the last four months or so, he's been pretty clean except for reports of the occasional partying and carousing, right up until the fight at the club this weekend.

Wait . . . he chartered the plane *himself?* I guess it's possible. Thanks to the detailed analysis of his life, I also know exactly how much he made in La Liga. With 150,000 euros per week, he could probably buy his own plane.

After the official report ends, the magazine clippings begin. He's with a different woman in every picture, appearing at red carpet events, parties, film festivals. One article in an Italian tabloid, which has a helpful English translation in the comments, claims he leaves heartbreak everywhere he goes.

I'm not sure how much damage a guy can do when he's a serial dater, but I'll give the journalist this: Gabriel Fortunato is devastating in a tuxedo. Some people were made for formal wear.

Not really something I can use, as the fans we're trying to target aren't the gala-attending crowd.

I spend the entire day at the front desk, skimming articles about Gabe and poking through his accounts. His Instagram posts are all action shots taken by professional photographers. There's nothing personal, very little text, and no responses to any comments. Given the other photos I've found online, I expected shirtless selfies, questionable parties, and lots of dudebros. His Twitter feed—what little there is—is mostly retweets of other players' messages and an occasional "Good game."

At five p.m., everyone starts to filter out of the office, telling me goodbye as they walk through the lobby. Mara, Javi, Arman, and Katie all leave together, but only Arman and Katie say good night. Mara and Javi are deep in a whispered conversation, so I tell myself they aren't actively ignoring me. And I believe it until they get in the elevator and Javi's gaze lingers on me. I wave goodbye, but he rolls his eyes and leans closer to say something in Mara's ear. Her jaw is set hard enough that I can see a muscle twitching.

I try not to let myself feel bad about it. I pounced when an opportunity presented itself. Mara would have done the same thing if the situations had been reversed.

A half hour later, Em sends me a text telling me not to wait for her. She's got lots of work to catch up on and is meeting a friend later for drinks. I walk out of the building alone, but as I turn right on Michigan Avenue the sun breaks between the buildings. And with it, I think, this is finally it—I've turned a corner in my life, I've been handed an opportunity, and I'm going to use it to make everything better.

I STAY UP LATE WATCHING YOUTUBE TUTORIALS ON HOW TO USE THE video editing software. It takes hours, but by one in the morning, I can cut video, lay in audio and text, and add music. I'm not a pro by any means, but I won't look like a total idiot when I try to edit the footage tomorrow.

Emma wasn't home by the time I climbed in bed with Watford curled into my knees, but she must have come in sometime, because the next morning, I find a fresh grapefruit on the kitchen counter and a sticky tab that says to meet her at the field at 8:30 a.m.—a half hour earlier than when William told me to be there. As I take a thirty-second shower, I wonder if he told me the wrong time.

That's got to be it. He wouldn't sabotage me intentionally.

I throw my hair into a bun that won't stay on the right side of messy, drag Watford out to the park to take the slowest dump possible, and speed walk to the closest bus stop so I can get on the first train out to Soldier Field. There's a line to climb on, and I'm mentally coaching the man in front of me to shuffle a little faster when my phone rings.

"Have you gotten on the bus yet?" Emma doesn't wait for an answer, powering on in a verbal rush that matches the physical rush of my morning. "If not, don't. Gabriel isn't answering his phone, and Scott thinks that means he's still asleep. Apparently, he's a very deep sleeper, so I need you to swing by his apartment and make sure he's on his way."

"Go to Gabe's apartment?"

"It'll take too long for one of us to come back from the stadium, but since you're close you can get him out here faster."

"Yeah. Of course." While I'm happy to do something that is actually helpful, the idea of going to Gabe's apartment isn't super appealing. What if I wake him up and he answers the door in his underwear?

Okay, that's a little appealing. And sort of a nice payback.

"I'll send a car to pick you up. See you in an hour."

And that's how I find myself standing outside Gabriel Fortunato's apartment door. I smooth my dress—a blue-and-white pin-striped A-line with a boat neck collar and cinched-in waist—over my hips, mostly to wipe my clammy hands.

I start with a soft *tap-tap-tap*, wait for a short eternity, and *tap-tap-tap* again. There's no answer. I check my phone, praying there's a text message from Em saying, *"Just kidding, he's here. Come back!"* No such luck.

I knock again, a little harder this time, and the door opens a tiny crack.

A squinting eye peers at me from below the chain. "Yes?" a feminine voice whisper-growls.

My eyes flick to the number on the door. Yep, right place. I'd mentally prepared to find Gabe in his underwear, but this is so much worse. Who is this girl? Is this his significant other? Hookup? There was nothing in his file about a girlfriend.

"Um, hi. I'm Maddie. From Velocity Marketing?" I fumble for my ID badge and hold it toward the crack in the door like a cop in a rerun of *Law & Order*. "I'm here to pick Gabe up for some social media videos we're working on today? About him?" *Obviously*. I give a nervous-sounding laugh. "Anyway, umm, is he here?"

She huffs an angry breath. "Yes." She fumbles with the chain for a second, then flings the door open. She's wearing a Fortunato jersey, and probably nothing else. I don't recognize her face from any of the tabloids, but even sleep-mussed and grouchy, she's beautiful.

"Come in," she says.

As she retreats, I get my first clue at her identity. Her legs are long and shapely, just like the girl in the silver dress from the bar fight.

I step into the dark entryway, half-closing the door behind me. Curtains block out some of the light from the huge windows, but I can still see a bit of Navy Pier and the lake beyond it. To my right, there's a good-size kitchen with four barstools tucked under a white-and-silver-speckled granite countertop. A grand piano fills the space where a kitchen table should be, and a leather couch forms a barrier to the rest of the living space. Blanket-covered feet hang over the armrest.

He's asleep on the couch? In his own apartment? Whoa. My mind tries to find explanations for why in the world he'd be there, but skids to a stop at an argument with the girl who answered the door. She looks the right height, has dark hair, is in his apartment. Yep. Definitely the girl who left with him after the bar fight.

Bar Girl leans down and shakes him. Gabe bolts upright, the tops of his bare shoulders flashing above the couch's back. She whispers something to him in what sounds like Italian, but that's just a guess on my part—according to his file, he speaks four languages fluently. His head whips toward me, eyes wide with shock.

"Morning," I say and immediately feel stupid for the too-cheery greeting. "You weren't answering your phone, so Emma sent me to get you."

He bursts off the couch and says, "Five minutes" before disappearing down the hall at a near run.

Bar Girl and I stare at each other awkwardly.

"Would you like to sit down?" She motions to the couch that five seconds ago Gabriel was asleep on. "Or coffee? I should make some for him anyway." She has a much heavier accent than he does, and it's sexy in a painfully recognizable way.

"Um. Yeah. Sure." At least that's better than standing here in a semi-dark room for five minutes, playing with my phone so I look like I'm doing something.

Bar Girl moves efficiently around the kitchen, popping little plastic cups into the Keurig, pulling down two travel mugs. Since she knows her way around the room, I think it's safe to assume she's probably not a hookup. An interminable amount of time (or three minutes) later she offers me a cup with a smile.

She's older than I initially thought, probably in her early twenties. I don't know why this surprises me. Gabe might only be nineteen, but he's rich, famous, and not painful to look at. I can't blame her for dating down.

"Thank you," I say.

She nods and goes back to the kitchen, rinsing the utensils in the sink and putting them in the dishwasher. Which definitely sends the vibe that she's here a lot. I'm about to strike up a conversation when Gabe flies down the hall, pulling an Adidas T-shirt over his head as he walks.

I gape at the body that could have posed for Michelangelo. Or was it Donatello? Everything from last year's humanities class flies out of my head when I'm presented with a real Italian masterpiece.

I look away but apparently not fast enough because Bar Girl sends me an amused simper. I take a swig of my coffee to break eye contact, but it scalds me worse than the shame heating my cheeks.

Bar Girl offers him the second cup of coffee. He says something quickly in Italian, presses a quick kiss to the side of her head, and he's striding toward the door.

"Bye. Thanks for this." I salute her with the travel mug and hurry after Gabe.

He's holding the elevator for me at the end of the hall, coffee in hand, face impatient.

Chill, bruh. You can wait five seconds for me, especially since everyone else has waited an hour for you.

The elevator doors slide closed, and he turns to face me. I swear the temperature inside the box drops to subzero. His shoulders are stiff, his mouth is hard.

"No one knows she was in my apartment, yes? Not your aunt, not my agent, not any media or paparazzi or anyone else."

Yikes. A little heavy on the intensity.

Then he runs his hand through his damp hair and looks at the floor. "I don't need everyone I love dragged through the mud with me, you know?"

Wow. He dropped the L-Bomb. Aww. That's sweet. It also means that Bar Girl is probably not a fling.

"Right. Of course. I can keep a secret."

The tension leaves his face, and his mouth softens. "Thank you for coming to get me. I forgot to charge my phone." He digs in his athletic bag and pulls out a battery pack. "It happens a lot."

"Maybe you should invest in an actual alarm clock." Really, Maddie? I cringe internally. He's an international soccer star. He could hire people to wake him up.

He gives a self-conscious laugh. "Probably."

"My brother has one that's solar powered so even if the electricity goes out it—you know—keeps running. And you don't ever have to worry about remembering to plug it in because . . . the sun." Just. Stop. Talking. I'm certain he's familiar with the sun and solar power, but my mouth keeps moving even though my brain has shut off.

"Huh."

And then I want to die. "Yep."

A black sedan idles outside the apartment complex. The driver acts like he's some sort of tour guide, explaining the sights of Chicago as we pass, so Gabe and I don't have to say anything to each other. He's busy on his still-charging phone, which gives me a chance to field Katie's nonstop stream of text messages.

Katie: So how's it going?

Me: He was late for training. I had to pick him up. Not a great start.

Katie: Not here either. The phones don't stop.

Katie: OMG. Mara. *teeth gritting emoji*

Me: What?

Katie: She hasn't *said* anything to me, but she's still stomping around. Hurry and come back to the office.

Katie: You ARE coming back to the office, right?

Katie: You better be coming back.

Katie: MADDIE!

As we near the stadium, Gabe turns toward me slightly and shows me his phone screen. There's a picture of a solar-powered alarm clock way nicer than the one Max has. "Do you think this is a good one?"

His shoulder is almost touching mine and he's asking my opinion on something. His nearness apparently overwhelms my senses because instead of saying something logical or even too much, all I manage is, "*Mmm.*"

He takes that as an affirmation and clicks the purchase button. "Thanks for the tip."

My brain scrambles for words. "I like that it has battery backup. You know. In case—"

"The sun stops shining?" His smile goes crooked.

"Or you forget to put it in a window."

"Which makes more sense than a nuclear winter."

"Right." I nod. "Or if the earth were to stop rotating."

He tilts his head to the side as he considers this. "Or a zombie apocalypse."

I'm a little bit charmed—and baffled—that he's playing along. "How could a zombie apocalypse stop the sun from shining?"

"It wouldn't. But you'd be hiding from the zombies, probably somewhere dark."

"Just *me* hiding?"

"Of course." He plucks the front of his team-branded workout shirt. "They couldn't catch me."

"So you'd run and leave me for zombie bait?"

He leans toward me, just a little bit, like he's about to share a secret. "If you're bait, then that means I'm setting up a zombie trap."

Ooo. He's quick. I guess I shouldn't be surprised, considering the back and forth we had yesterday. "What if I—"

The sedan lurches a little, and I fling my arm out to stop myself from flying forward. Through the window over Gabe's shoulder, the spaceship-topped stadium looms.

"Excuse me," the driver interrupts. "Is this the entrance I'm looking for?"

"Yes. You can drop me off here," Gabe says, already unbuckling his seat belt. "You'll have to check in at the front desk, Madeline."

"All right. See you inside."

He hops out of the car, already moving at a jog while he looks over his shoulder and waves goodbye. It's sort of endearing.

Fingers crossed that Emma, William, and I can make the rest of the world see that.

CHAPTER

EIGHT

THERE'S NO FILM CREW. NO MAKEUP TEAM. NO LIGHTING OR discussion of Gabe's good side. I don't know why I imagined I'd be watching him run in slow motion while his hair was artfully tossed by a wind machine—none of that was in Emma's plan. But for some reason, I did expect it to feel more staged.

"The average person wants to believe that, with enough effort, they won't be average forever," Emma says as she points out where she wants me to stand while I film Gabe. William and I are supposed to get footage on our phones from different angles. Later we'll edit and post the shots that are the most compelling. "We want to sell people on the fact that Gabriel Fortunato is just like them."

But he's not. He's not even average by MLS standards.

He literally runs laps around his teammates. He's faster, focused, intense in every exercise. He silently beats himself up—hands on hips, head down, face frustrated—when he's unhappy with his performance. But he never holds his teammates to the same standards, giving high fives and fist bumps and otherwise celebrating their successes.

I'm a little bit amazed at the ease at which he goes through his day, simply pretending three people aren't filming him the whole time. He laughs, he jokes, he's actually likable.

"Who's the best Italian on our team?" he asks the trainer spotting him on some weird balance and coordination exercise that involves standing on one foot on a mini-tramp while juggling a soccer ball with the other. He carries on a conversation like this activity doesn't require any concentration.

"You're the only one, Gabe." The trainer's face scrunches.

"The One. And. Only." He cheers for himself, then flicks the ball over his head and stalls it on the top of his foot.

We all laugh because it's a horrible joke.

I don't want to be impressed, but I am. Darn it. How can someone be egotistical one second but coachable in the next? Somehow, it all works together to be *enchanting*, and I don't think it's all an act for the camera. His friends seem genuinely pleased to work out with him as they rotate through their different schedules, pre-practice conditioning, tape, and massage.

Emma's smiling. William seems happy. They all see how this version of Gabriel Fortunato could be the perfect spokesman, the guy you want to wear your expensive shoes or watches or drive your fancy cars.

Just before eleven, the whole team—at least those who aren't with their national teams competing for the Gold Cup—meets together for footwork drills on the outdoor field. I shade my eyes against the bright glare of sunlight and notice that one silhouette stands at least a head taller than all the others. Recognition hits me like static shock. It's Super Tall. One of the other guys from the beach.

He's jogging toward the goal because, hello, of course the guy who is six foot ten is the goalie. He jolts when he sees me, stopping midstride. I give a Queen Elizabeth–style wave. He stares at me for a second, then calls Gabe over and they have a quick conversation with their heads bent toward each other. As if it were choreographed, they both look over at me, then at each other, and burst out laughing.

What's the likelihood they're not talking about me? Laughing at me? I've been the punch line of a lot of jokes. *Giraffes can't dance, but Maddie sure tries.* Haha. I've learned how to handle most of that crap, but knowing two grown men—even if one of them is only nineteen—are making fun of me is an extra-hard slap to the face. My cheeks sting with heat, my eyes burn, my throat aches worse than it did when I swigged Bar Girl's nuclear coffee.

I turn my back to the field so they can't see the devastation on my face and realize that Emma's only a few feet away. She's smiling, hands tucked into the pockets of a business jumpsuit thing. I tried it on but couldn't get comfortable with the idea of getting naked to pee. Sitting in your bra in a public bathroom apparently doesn't faze her.

What does it take to be that secure in your own skin?

She must feel my eyes because she looks over at me, eyebrows lifting over a pair of giant glasses as if expecting a question. So I come up with one. "When are we breaking for lunch?"

"About thirty minutes or so. We're not allowed to go into the lunchroom with the team, but there are plenty of places nearby where you can grab something."

"Sounds like a plan."

"Are you getting any good footage?"

I open my phone and scroll through the videos I've captured, none longer than thirty seconds, and show her the one I filmed while lying on the ground. It's cropped so you can only see Gabe from the calves down. His feet move so quickly as he dribbles the ball between barriers that it looks like it's in fast-forward.

"That's perfect. Good work, Mads." She squeezes my forearm, and her touch works like a balm to my humiliation. "Tell me about your car ride here."

"Nothing much to tell. Our driver talked almost the whole way."

Emma doesn't say anything for a moment too long, and I can't read her expression behind her dark lenses. "The most important aspect of this job is building open, honest relationships. With clients. With reporters. With influencers. I think, given your history with Gabe, that you'll have a better chance at that than I do."

The disappointment in her tone replaces the temporary balm with sandpaper. "Yeah."

"You had half an hour to talk to him one-on-one, and you didn't take the opportunity to see if there was *anything* we don't already know that will work in our favor?"

I don't think zombie apocalypse alarm clocks is what she's asking for. The brief interaction Gabe and I had in the elevator bubbles on my tongue, but I bite down on the words. I'm not sure why he felt it was important to hide Bar Girl's sleepover at his apartment, but I don't want to betray him right away.

"You're right." I nod gamely.

No excuse. No explanation. If there's one thing I've learned from Max, who is almost always right, it's that if you don't give him something to argue with, he can't. It appears to work on Emma, too.

She wipes at the makeup under her glasses, though as far as I can tell, her face is impeccable. It's a tired gesture. And a frustrated one.

"The team is bringing in some children from the local hospital to meet with the players after lunch," she says. "William and I are going to head back to the office, but I want you to stay. Film Gabe interacting with the kids. I need just two or three quality stills and thirty seconds of video of him giving hugs and signing autographs. Fans love to see their players' soft sides, and it's great for the team and sponsors to see Gabe giving back to the community. Can you handle that?"

"Of course. No problem."

"Set up a time to talk about his passions and his goals. Get the answers and find at least one thing we can add to our content calendar."

My aunt doesn't give me suggestions on how to make any of that happen, and I don't ask. This is a challenge, and she wants me to figure it out on my own.

I just hope I can.

I EAT MY LUNCH IN THE TUNNEL UNDERNEATH THE STADIUM, BAL-ancing my drink on a cement half-pillar while I devour the last few bites of my Italian roast beef sandwich from a restaurant up the street. Something about watching someone else work out stoked my appetite, and I can't get the greasy peppers and onions down fast enough.

"Giordano's?" a voice asks behind—and above—me.

I turn and look up to find Super Tall. The Goalie. The Friend Who Laughed at Me. I could give him a hundred titles, but I can't quite place his name.

"If you're going to eat at a famous pizza restaurant," he contin-ues, leaning a shoulder against the wall beside me, "you've really got to stick with what they're famous for."

"But the sandwich was delicious." I ball the wrapper up and toss it into the garbage can next to the locker room door. "Good bread, good meat, good toppings."

Super Tall nods his agreement. "Don't let Gabe hear you say that." He holds out his giant paw for me to shake. "Sebastian Morales, but most people call me Seb. I'm Gabe's friend."

"Madeline McPherson—"

"We've met before." He gives me a playful wink and a wide smile. His front teeth overlap just a little, and his thick tousled hair adds at least four inches to his height. He'd be flirt-worthy if I was maybe three or four years older. "Gabe says you're an intern at Velocity?"

I know Gabe talked to Seb about me because I saw it, but maybe it was more than just rehashing my crash at the beach.

"I am." I wave to the badge the team gave me when I walked in.

"This your first year?"

"Yeeeaaah?" I stretch it into a question. There's a wryness to his body language. Like he doesn't quite believe me. "Why do I feel like you're checking my story?"

"Oh, I am. No offense intended."

"None taken, I guess?"

He folds his arms across his chest, still looking down at me with an inquisitive smirk. "You can't be too careful. Especially when it comes to Gabe."

"You mean because of the flirty stalkers and fainting fangirls?"

Seb nods slowly. "And others." He has a super-deep voice to go along with his height, and it goes a little gruff on that phrase.

"Well . . ." I hold my hands out to my sides. "Did I pass your test?"

"You passed *mine* when you showed up here with the other Velocity folks, but Gabe's a little slower to trust than I am. Bad experiences that I'm sure you've heard about."

Actually, I haven't. There's nothing about trust issues in his file. And—*ugh!*—it's not like I took the time I had this morning to get to know him. Why did we talk about a potential zombie apocalypse instead of his life history?

Because that feels oh-so-natural. *Hi! I'm Maddie. We've known each other for five minutes. Please expose your darkest secrets.*

I must be doing something with my face because Seb's expression melts. "You *don't* know." He blows out a long breath. "After the World Cup and the way everything went down with the fans and that announcer—"

A high-pitched shriek echoes down the tunnel toward us. It's a happy noise I recognize, even if it is ear piercing. My little brother, Cube, used to screech like that when he was really excited. There are two women, each pushing a wheelchair, another carrying a toddler on her hip, and a man pulling two children along in a wagon. A handful of staffers lead another twenty or so kids and parents toward us.

"Later," Seb says, breaking away from me. "Hey, crew! Are you here to meet some soccer players?"

The child being carried holds up her bony arms and says, "You're Seb! You're Seb!" She flings herself out of her parents' arms and into Seb's. He catches her and slings her onto his hip like he's totally accustomed to it.

I step back, letting Seb lead the group into the locker room. It's a long narrow room, flanked on both sides with open-faced wooden lockers and low benches. All the waiting players, including Gabe, grin as the children walk in. A bunch of older kids break directly toward him.

Gift bags are handed out. The kids don their team-branded hats,

T-shirts, and foam fingers. Gabe chats and laughs and uses a black Sharpie to sign sleeves and backs and, on one occasion, an arm. He's adorable and engaging and so painfully sweet as he drops onto one knee to accept a hug from a kindergarten-size girl in a pink beanie. He asks her name and laughs at something she says, and I realize I'm practically the human equivalent of a heart-eyes emoji.

This is exactly why I want to work in sports business.

Two years ago, I volunteered at one of Emma's Children's Miracle Network events, and I realized that organizing events and facilitating opportunities for athletes to give back to their fans, to their communities, even in small ways, would be the most amazing career. Every decision I've made since then was to get me on the right path: follow Em's footsteps, get a degree in sports administration at UNC, intern at Velocity, and then work here long term.

And right now, I'm mentally straying.

Watching the combination of Gabe's broad, athletic shoulders and the gentle way he accepts hugs and listens to little voices is so attractive that my brain has stalled out. I'm clearly not the only person suffering from the Gabriel Fortunato Effect. Grown women, some probably old enough to be his mother, blush and swoon when he smiles in their general direction. When he stoops down to sign an autograph for a little boy in a wheelchair, the two women standing behind him exchange a look and fan themselves.

Okay, Self. You are not a member of his fan club. Get to work.

One of the mothers asks for a picture and Gabe ends up with a little boy on his shoulders and a little girl on each side. I step next to the mom and get a couple shots. Gabe's smile fades for a second but pops back into place before the cameras click again.

He lifts the little boy off his shoulders and hands the child to his very grateful mom, then he strides over to where I'm standing.

"Madeline. A word, please?" His expression is closed, jaw clenched.

I'm guessing that whatever he has to say isn't for everyone to hear. I sort of expect him to whisk me outside, but instead he steps close, using his body as a barrier to separate us from the crowd. Eyes widen in our direction, and I'm sure people speculate as to why he's close-talking.

"Is there something I can help you with?" I loop my fingers through the lanyard around my neck, hoping that onlookers will realize it's an official badge.

He bends toward me, hand low on my back, urging me closer so that he can whisper in my ear, and my mind blanks with his proximity.

"Don't take any more pictures."

"What?" I lean away, needing to watch his lips move so I can process what he's saying.

"No pictures of me and the children."

My face crinkles in confusion. "That's *why* I'm here."

"Just . . ." He pauses and runs a hand through his hair. "Just let it be about the kids today, okay?"

"The rest of the team is taking pictures. And my aunt expects—"

"Please." He shoots a look over his shoulder where a half circle of children with a soccer ball is forming near us. Their mothers watch us with interest. "I'll make it up to you—get you something even better."

Seb's words from the tunnel combine with what Aunt Em said earlier. I've got to build a relationship with Gabe, and that's never going to happen if I do exactly the opposite of what he asks.

"Okay." I lick my lips, already nervous about how I'm going to explain this to Emma.

A real smile, not the too-cheesy one he puts on for the children, breaks across his face. "I'll text you details tonight."

And then he's off. He swipes the ball and starts to juggle it with Cirque du Soleil skill, rolling it across his shoulders to catch it with the outside of the foot, bouncing it from knee to knee before flicking it up to stall on his head.

"Show off!" Seb yells from across the room.

Everyone, including Gabe, laughs. He slows the ball's roll and drops it at the feet of a frail-looking boy who bursts into applause.

It's all so golden—everything Emma wanted to capture—but I didn't get any of it. Nerves curl into a tight bundle beneath my skin, tingling with anxiety. Did I make a huge mistake?

Nine

B Y THE TIME I ARRIVE AT THE OFFICE BUILDING, MY BRAIN IS full of possibilities for ways I can edit the footage, what music would set off Gabe's speed, hashtags Emma might not have considered. Basically, anything that would make her forget the photos I *didn't* get.

All of the interns are huddled around the front desk, talking to Katie, purses and laptop bags slung over shoulders like they're about to leave for the day.

"Maddie!" Katie pushes through the crowd and throws her arms around me. She's at least seven inches shorter than I am, but it's a hug that's as pleasant as it is surprising. "I'm so glad you're back."

"Why? So I can manage the desk tomorrow?"

She nods like a bobblehead. "Yes!"

Katie's laugh is contagious. The *yuk-yuk-yuk* sound is so unexpected from someone so dainty. Everyone laughs, which feels great considering how awful things were yesterday.

"I'm totally kidding. I missed having you around today. And it's my birthday!" She grabs a different grocery tote. This one is a little fancier, with multicolored quilted pockets on the outside. "We were going to head down to an early dinner at Aster Hall to celebrate. Come with us!"

She practically sticks a pin in the other interns' bubble of happiness. Mara deflates, face going dead, no smile whatsoever. Javi's a little slower to follow, as if remembering he's on Team Mara. Arman's head whips to check his friends' expressions and then back to me in a painfully obvious way. His mouth quirks apologetically.

"You know, I actually have to upload all this video to the server." I try to pretend I'm oblivious to the uncomfortable haze floating around us, but it's like one of my brothers' farts—invisible but impossible to ignore. "If it goes really fast, then I'll meet you guys. But happy birthday!"

I have no intention of meeting any of them, and they all know it.

"Do you want me to order something for you?" Katie asks.

I'm already edging toward the secret door. "I'm good. Thanks, though." Once it clicks shut after me, I can only imagine what they're saying. It's clear that Mara and her minion, Javi, consider me an enemy. Arman seems cautiously neutral, but everything about him is understated. He's one of those giant guys with a really soft voice. The few times we've spoken, I felt like I needed to lean in to hear him better. Javi is completely opposite, extra loud to make up for his smaller stature.

Dropping into my desk chair, I try to sort through every interaction, every conversation, anything that might have made them dislike me. I know Mara was upset that I got to work on the Fortunato account, but it wasn't like I had a choice in the matter. She can't possibly blame me for being in the wrong place at the right time.

Or maybe she's just evil.

"Hey," a voice says behind me.

I spin my chair around and find Katie hovering in my cubicle's doorway. She's taken off her giant cardigan, showing her super-toned Iron Woman arms, and she's pulled her hair out of her bun so it's all messy beach waves. She made the office-to-evening transition effortlessly.

"I'm sad they made you feel unwelcome. This is *my* birthday celebration, and I want you to come."

"I honestly have so much that I need to get done. Maybe we can go out tomorrow or another day? We should celebrate your birthday for a whole week!" My smile feels more like the expression you'd make after biting a lemon instead of something your face does naturally.

Katie reads it, her eyes filling with pity. "Listen." She stops and goes up onto her tiptoes to scan the rest of the floor. There are a few lights on in the junior executives' offices, but the cubes around us are empty. "I know why Mara's mad."

"Because I'm working on Gabe's account."

"No. It's not that." She hurries to add, "It's not *just* that. This is her third year as an intern, and she's pissed that you got onto a huge, high-profile account so fast. She's never gotten to work on anything with this much visibility, and she feels like you took away something she earned."

"But she's already got way more responsibility than we do. I know she pulled together all the information from the surveys for the ticket-pricing account."

Katie's nose squishes up. "Ticket-pricing research versus daily interaction with a hot professional athlete?" She makes a balancing scale with her hands and lets one side drop to her leg. "Mara thinks you got the Fortunato account because your aunt is giving you preferential treatment."

"No way." But then the words bite and hold on. "I mean . . . my aunt thinks he'll work better with someone he already knows. It could have been you. It could have been Mara. It just happened that I met him my first weekend in the city."

I think about my bike crash, the humiliation I felt. I can't bear to give someone who already hates me—for sort of a good reason—any more ammunition.

"You've got this weird look on your face." Katie walks the rest of the way into my cubicle and hops up onto the desktop. "Girl, spill."

"Aren't people waiting for you?"

"They can wait for a minute."

"It's honestly so embarrassing." I swallow over the lump in the back of my throat and push on. "On the way home from work on Friday, Watford escaped from me, and Gabe and his friends captured him on the beach. Anyway, Gabe was . . . nice. Even after Watford ate their soccer ball. Then in the breakfast meeting yesterday, I knocked over a big stack of cups, and Gabe realized who I was."

Katie sits silent for a few seconds, mulling over this information. "This almost makes me want to get a dog."

She's a little like Max, always finding a silver lining in the dark cloud of my day, and it makes me feel better. "You can borrow Watford anytime."

"I will take you up on that. Don't tease." She hops off the desk, realizing that the other interns are probably waiting for her. "Also, is it okay if I tell Mara about you and Fortunato? How you met?"

"Yeah, of course. Please do, if you think it will help."

"It might. She'll just realize you're the luckiest girl alive."

"I totally classify losing my aunt's dog at the beach and dropping cups in a meeting as evidence of good luck."

Katie half pirouettes out my door. "Good things come in unlikely packages."

And even though she leaves to go to a party where I wasn't welcome, I think maybe she's right.

THERE'S A DETAILED SET OF DIRECTIONS ABOUT HOW TO LOAD VIDEOS to Velocity's secure server, make shared versus private folders, and create a password to access them when you're out of the office. All the safety steps make sense because Velocity keeps a file on every one of their clients, and I know Gabriel's issues are a pimple compared to the plague that infects some of the other celebrities. That kind of muck should be kept in a dragon-protected vault. Sexual harassment charges. Fraud. Tax violations. You name it, Emma's got clients who have done it.

Once everything is loaded, I play with the editing system for so long that I lose track of time. Em pops her head in my cubicle at six, pride on her face. "You're still here?"

"Just teaching myself how to edit." I'm a little nervous to show her what I've done, but I pull up the video of Gabe's feet. Some track star pinned a commercial he did for a shoe company to his timeline, and I figured I could follow that example. I've set the video to an electronica song that matches the natural rhythm of his body.

"That's perfect." She squeezes my shoulder. "Here's how you can take it to the next level: get him talking about the years of work that he's put into moving that fast. People love hearing a professional athlete's ability wasn't a gift from God."

I don't contradict her even though I'm positive Gabe's talent is a genetic fluke.

"Find a time to interview him. Get simple answers for now, and then we can rephrase whatever he says and feed it back to him for video."

"Great." My enthusiasm is fake, but I'm not going to get an excellent letter of recommendation by whining about assignments.

Emma reaches into her purse and pulls out some big gold hoop earrings and takes off her diamond studs. "I'm grabbing dinner with an agent tonight. Do you mind walking Watty? He's been trapped inside so much lately."

"No problem. I'll take him now." I disconnect my phone from the computer and delete all the videos.

"Thanks, Mads. We'll have dinner together later this week. Anything you want."

"Mon Ami Gabi?" The steak frites is my absolute favorite. Emma probably has it all the time, since it's the restaurant in her building, but I don't mind repeating the meal.

"Steak frites again?" Her exasperation is fake. I know she loves them as much as I do. "I guess I can make the sacrifice."

She waits while I shut down my computer and grab my bag, and we walk out together. There's no one in the lobby now, and as we wait outside the elevator doors she says, "I saw your fire again today."

"My fire?" Like the fire of embarrassment in my face?

"I saw the moment you had an epiphany and lay down on the field, totally ignoring the fact that you were in a dress, so you could get that video of his feet. Then you came straight back here and put your idea into action." She grabs my hand, just like she used to when I was little, and gives it a hard squeeze. "I never doubted that you'd be good at this, Mads. But today you proved you could be great."

As the elevator doors slide shut, I check my phone. There's no message from Gabe. If he blows me off, what am I going to do?

MMA'S WORDS ARE NOT AN EGO BOOST. THEY LAND LIKE A PIANO across my shoulders. The weight of wanting to prove her right and everyone else wrong is crushing. I have to keep reminding myself that I *can* do this job. I have fire. Emma saw it. I just need William, the other interns, and my family to see it, too.

I should have talked to her as we left the office about not getting any footage of Gabe with the kids from the children's hospital. *Later*, I promise myself. After he texts me tonight and I have something concrete to offer Emma as an alternative.

A walk with Watford and a carb-heavy dinner will help me figure everything out. I head north toward the lily pond by the conservatory instead of toward the beach. Watford is so grateful to be out of the apartment that there's a bounce to his step, and his stubby little tail is extra waggly. Emma has a professional dog walker who comes in Monday through Thursday to let him go potty and take a turn around Lincoln Park, but it's really not enough exercise for an eighty-five-pound monster dog.

He bounds toward a bush sniffing happily, dribbling three drops of pee onto it, and then trots away. I wish his joy were contagious, that a good mood were a thing you could catch. Wouldn't it be amazing if something as simple as a walk in the park, a nap in the sun, and a cuddle with someone you love would be enough to alter your perception of a day? This trip to the pond needs to shake my thoughts around, so that maybe the good ones can surface.

What I really need is someone to help me see this whole situation clearly. And I have a person in mind who owes me a million hours of listening, since I've nodded my head and *mm-hmm*'d for every plot and character problem for as long as I understood those words.

My mom picks up on the first ring. "Maddie! Hi, honey! I sure miss your face. How is everything going?"

I smile at the real pleasure in her voice. Despite our different ideas for my future, I know she loves me. "I have a nemesis."

"*You?*" She sounds a little echoey, and when I hear something clicking in the background, I realize it's the overloud blinker in our ancient Camry. "I don't believe it. What could you have possibly done in such a short period of time to earn someone's ire?"

Ire. Only my mom.

I give her a very brief rundown of what happened with Mara and a very edited version of how I met Gabe. "And now," I say as I force Watford onto the path that heads past the Lincoln Park Zoo instead of toward Lake Michigan—he seems a little confused, but he plods on, still happy to be outside—"she's turned into the villain of my summer internship."

"Oh, sweetie. The best villains have justifiable reasons for being awful. You have to remember that this Mara person is the hero of her own life."

"It's hard to do that when she's such a—"

"*Shh!*" she hisses before I can even get the first letter past my lips. "Milo's in the car."

"Sorry." Then it's my turn to laugh. "What's up, Cube?"

My little brother literally growls like a rabid animal. "I told you not to call me that anymore!"

Max came up with the nickname "Cube" because our little brother's real name is Milo Matthew McPherson, and he's the third McPherson with an *M* name. It was really cute when Cube was a toddler because he was supper chubby; the name just sorta fit. He's gotten taller and leaner the last few years, looking more like a Mini Max than anything else, but he'll always be Cube in my head.

"You did tell me," I say, as Watford leaps into a bush. I see the white tail of a rabbit disappear into the distance. Watford whines for a second as I hold him back. "Wish you were here to help me with Watty."

"I wish I was too, because that would mean *no more math camp.*" His voice gets really loud at the end of the sentence, and I can imagine him leaning between the seats to yell into the phone.

"Hush and sit back," my mom reprimands. "And put your seat belt back on."

I give myself a mental high five because I know my family so well. "Is someone being mean to you?"

"No," he mumbles. "It's just boring."

This moody thing he's doing is almost funny because I know it's an act. There are days when Milo forgets he's trying to behave like his older siblings and totally gives in to being a kid. I like him better when he's all *pew-pew* sound effects and Lego battles, but I can't hold on to baby Cube forever.

"I know, but math camp is good for you."

"How would you know?" He sounds farther away now, probably having been smacked in the chest so he'd obey. "Mom never made you go."

"Everyone has different gifts, Milo. Maddie's might not be in math, but she's amazing at other things. Like . . . teaching dance to toddlers."

I try not to let that sting. "Yeah. Well, Cube, just try to make it fun."

"Whatever."

My mom and I sigh at the same time, then we both giggle.

"We're headed into the store. Call me later if you want to talk more."

"Thanks, Mom. Love you guys."

There's a weird, guttural noise in the background, but I don't know what it is until I hear Mom yell, "Milo! How many times have I told you belching is not appropriate?"

"I was telling Maddie that I love her in burp language."

"Back atcha, Cube."

We hang up as I reach the gates of the Alfred Caldwell Lily Pool. It isn't one of Chicago's most famous locations, but it's certainly one of my favorites. As much as I love Lincoln Park, Lake Michigan, the energy of the Magnificent Mile, and all the urban offerings, I find my way to this quiet, secluded oasis at least once on every visit to the city. My dad introduced me to it, sharing his reverence for the arching trees and slow-moving water. If I equated all the adults in my life to a particular location, Emma would be Chicago—all flashy and bright and busy. My mom would obviously be Normal—constant, predictable, and the place I'll always go home to. And Dad would be the Lily Pool—quiet, unshakable, a little rugged.

For as much as I want to be like my aunt—all go all the time—I know I do my best thinking in quiet places. I take a deep breath, excited to worship at the church of nature.

The entrance has a big, metal gate that makes it look like someplace the public isn't invited, but I think that's part of its charm—a man-made gateway to a natural wonderland.

And then I notice the sign: NO DOGS ALLOWED.

Inside jokes, intern dinners, and now the pond. It seems the theme for the day is "Places Maddie will be left out of." Watford looks at me with mournful eyes and bumps his head against my thigh. I hear the "I'm so sorry" in his contact.

"It's okay, buddy." I scratch behind his floppy ears. "We're not going to let this get us down, right?"

As we walk back to Emma's apartment, I decide the best way to salvage this day is with cake.

Everything's better with cake.

CHAPTER

ELEVEN

MY PHONE BUZZES AT MIDNIGHT.

I've spent the last several hours splicing together video to keep my mind off the fact that Gabe hasn't kept his freaking promise. Max and I exchanged no fewer than a dozen text messages on the subject. He bet *if* Gabe actually followed through it would be really late.

Looks like my bro is a genius in human nature, too.

The text says, Late lunch tomorrow at Moretti's after practice?

I know exactly who it's from, but for some inexplicable reason I can't help myself from responding:

Me: Who is this?

Him: Do you always respond to texts from strangers late at night?

I smirk.

Me: Did you expect me not to respond?

The three little dots cycle for a while before he answers:

Him: Maybe.

It sure took him a long time to come up with a one-word answer, but it only takes me a second to type a much longer response.

Me: You texted me at midnight *hoping* I wouldn't answer? Do you not want to get together tomorrow? If not, that's okay. We can figure out a plan in the next couple of days. But I need to have something great to show my aunt or I'm going to get into huge trouble for not taking pictures of you with the kids.

And then William will hate me and then he won't write me a good letter of recommendation and I won't get into UNC.

Him: You send long texts.

In my head, he sounds petulant. I imagine him draped across his leather couch, shirt off, one arm tucked behind his head, bicep flexed.

Wait . . . what? Slow your roll, Imagination. It must be tired because my mind just took a super-inappropriate jump.

Sorry, I text back. I mean it for both the long message and remembering him shirtless this morning. I'm glad no one can see me because I'm flushed, and the back of my neck is hot. I shouldn't be thinking about him—especially not like *that*. Plus, there was a girl wearing only his jersey in his apartment. That thought dumps an imaginary bucket of cold water on my brain.

Him: Moretti's at three o'clock. Go through the alley door.

I wonder what that's all about, but he sends me an address that's not far from my aunt's apartment.

Me: See you then.

Him: Sweet dreams.

I'm blushing. Why am I blushing? It's not like he knows I was just thinking about him. Shirtless.

I don't respond to his text, but I also can't concentrate on anything else. So I send my brother a message:

I'm attracted to someone totally inappropriate.

My phone rings instantly. "Talk to me, Goose." Max has a deep and abiding love for movie references, but this is one I know because he says it all the time.

"*Top Gun* is a horrible movie."

"Not disagreeing, but it's a great line."

I can't argue with that, so I spill everything. I leave out the bit about shirtless Gabe this morning—there are some things that even your older brother–best friend doesn't need to know. But I don't hold back on how cute Gabe was with the kids.

"I was . . . melty."

"That's not a real word." Max laughs. It's the sound of holidays and Saturday mornings. It's the sound of home. "But I get the sentiment."

I climb under the frothy duvet on the guest bed, and Watford jumps up after me. "What do I do?"

"Nothing," Max says emphatically. "You do not get involved with a guy like Gabriel Fortunato, even if he makes you *melty*." He gags a little to punctuate that sentence.

"Of course not. He's a client. There are probably rules. Ethics. Bad . . . karma?"

Max snorts. "You're not convincing me. So let me convince you: You've already made an enemy. How much more is this Mara chick going to hate you if she thinks you're only on the Fortunato account because you've got a thing for him?"

"With the fire of a thousand suns?"

He's silent for a minute. "Are you quoting *Ten Things I Hate about You* or *Taming of the Shrew*?"

"Neither. Both. I don't know." I roll my eyes, even though no one but Watford can see me. "How do you remember this stuff?"

"It's not like I'm trying. Some things just get stuck in there."

"There" meaning his giant brain. And he's not bragging. When he was younger, he hated to read because he said stories got lodged in his mind and left him with too much to think about.

"Next question—"

"You have more questions?" My voice shifts octaves on the last word and Watford lifts his head to give me the stink eye.

"Would having a crush on him stop you from doing your best work?"

I don't answer right away, suddenly doubting my own motives. Was the real reason I didn't take pictures of Gabe with the kids because I agreed that exploiting sick children was wrong or because I wanted him to like me? "Uggghhhh."

"I'll take that as a yes." He sounds so self-satisfied that I immediately jump on the defensive.

"It's not a yes. It's just not a no."

Max does his disbelieving cough-laugh. "Go to bed, Mads."

"Will do. Love you, Bro."

"Ditto."

I shake my head against my pillow. "That's from that Patrick Swayze movie Mom loves," I say.

"It wasn't a reference to *Ghost*. It was just a goodbye."

When he hangs up, I realize that for the first time in my life I'm a little homesick. That thought, instead of anything work related, lulls me to sleep.

I'M SLATED TO WORK THE FRONT DESK THE NEXT MORNING, BUT Katie insists on joining me until lunch. She drags a big box of tabloids and another chair to sit beside me.

"If you get wrapped up in something Fortunato-related, then I can take the phones." She pulls out a stack of European magazines and plops them on the long tabletop. "And if I get sucked into a mind-numbing whirlpool of beautiful people, then you can pull me out."

For the past two years, I haven't put friendships very high on my priority list. There are girls from my high school dance team that I hang out with every now and then, and a couple of them were pretty disappointed when I decided not to try out for the team for our senior year. Even though they were my friends, I've never felt like any of them could be the *one* friend that I texted about every single thing. Partially because I've always had Max. If there was anything funny or important, he was my go-to. And if the issues were too uncomfortable to share with him, I always went to my mom.

Being here in the city, away from my family, has made me feel like I'm missing out on something. Maybe I need a friend who doesn't share my DNA?

I can't restrain my grin from Katie, both because she's becoming my friend and because she pretends to hate combing through the gossips. "You totally love this part of our job."

"I do. It's sort of gross, but the eye candy, the dresses, and the makeup tips are so much better than making copies and getting coffee." She holds up both hands. "Sorry."

"It's fine." Mostly because she's not wrong. I'm happy that I'm an awesome coffee-getter, but I'll be happier if I can prove that I'm also a fabulous video editor, social media wizard, and intern publicist.

My second day at the front desk is so much less hectic than the first. I don't know if it has to do with my skills improving or if it's Katie's company, but I find plenty of time to work on Fortunato-related projects on Patty's computer, scribbling a list of possible questions, and I don't hang up on anyone at all.

At two, Mara shows up. She's wearing a summer sweater and pin-striped pants with enormous, flared bottoms, and her long, glossy hair hangs over her shoulder in an intricate braid. I instantly have outfit envy. It's not that I look bad in Aunt Emma's clothes, but they don't belong to me. Mara isn't shopping in someone else's closet. She just looks this good all the time.

"Arman is busy, so I offered to take the afternoon shift." She delivers the sentence without any inflection. She's either not thrilled with her volunteer position, or she's still doing her best to hate my guts.

I decide to play dumb. "It's nice of you to help."

She shrugs. "Katie was stuck out here all day yesterday and this morning with you. And Javi offered, but he strikes up random conversations with strangers."

"Oh, I totally understand that." I save my work in the editing program and offer her the chair with a flourish. "Anything I can get you before I leave?"

"No."

Well, all righty then. Should I try to explain? Probably not. I don't know that it will do any good, since Katie already tried to smooth things over for me.

Something my mom said yesterday echoes in my ears. Everyone is the hero of their own story. I guess that makes me the villain of Mara's. Have I unintentionally derailed her summer internship plans?

Her loss is my gain. Ugh. What a horrible thought. What a *villainous* thought.

I decide not to chat her up. Even though it bothers me to know that someone dislikes me, no one likes to hear the bad guy monologue about their reasons.

As I step into the elevator, I look over the list of questions I wrote for my meeting with Gabe. They're good questions. Leading questions. I smooth out my hair and take a deep breath.

I can have a clear conversation with Gabriel Fortunato and not act like an idiot.

Probably.

Twelve

ORETTI'S IS A TINY STOREFRONT ON CLARK STREET NOT FAR from my aunt's apartment. I've probably walked past it a dozen times and never noticed it wedged between a yoga studio and fancy soap and lotion shop.

I intend to walk through the front door like a normal person, but the little blue-and-white sign is flipped to CLOSED, so I guess I'm stuck following Gabe's directions. As I head toward the break between the buildings, a silver Ferrari whips past me and turns into the alley.

Gabe climbs out, phone in hand, reflective sunglasses hiding his eyes.

"Is it legal to park here?" There isn't a NO PARKING sign, but the last thing I need is his car getting towed while I'm supposed to be meeting him for an early dinner.

"Yes," he says, with a laugh. "At least for me." He opens an all-metal door set into the brick wall, and when I hesitate to walk into Moretti's kitchen, he sighs and leads the way.

Once inside, I'm overwhelmed with the mouthwatering fragrance of garlic and baking bread. Stems of herbs—drying basil, rosemary, and oregano—hang from a rack lining the ceiling, and a pristine, busy kitchen fills a space larger than I imagined for a restaurant this size.

"Gabe!" a woman about my mother's age cheers when she sees us. She rushes over, plastic glove-covered hands held out to the sides, as she offers her cheeks for him to kiss.

He does immediately, speaking in Italian, gesturing to me. Whatever he says earns me a wide grin in greeting, and she ushers us to a tiny bistro table shoved into a nook that might once have been a closet.

"The back table, huh?" I wedge into the chair that can only slide a handful of inches from the wall. When Gabe sits down, his knee knocks against mine, and it takes a second to arrange my legs so that they aren't touching his. My feet rest on the base of the pedestal with his straddling mine. Even with the width of the table separating us, there's barely enough space for two plates.

"You should see me and Scott try to fit."

The image of Scott's bulk and Gabe's body smashed in here together makes me smile. "You eat here a lot?"

"As often as I can." Then his expression shutters. "Don't tell anyone that. I'd like it to—"

"Stay private. I understand."

The woman sets down two glasses of water, a wood platter covered in cheese, salami, and bruschetta, and a pile of what looks like eggplant, then disappears without saying a word.

Gabe immediately creates a miniature sandwich, while I dig in my wallet for my folded piece of paper. There isn't really a lot of space on the table, so I leave it on my lap. I'll start with a harmless question and hope that the other topics come up naturally.

"How do you like Chicago so far?"

"Is that an official question, or are you just making conversation?" he asks without looking at me.

Not as harmless as I imagined. "I guess that depends on your answer."

"If I hate Chicago and want nothing more than to return to Italy, you'll only tell me to lie." He shoots me a chilly sideways glance. "Why don't you just tell me what you want me to say?"

"Why don't you tell me the truth, and we can go from there?"

"I love Chicago. It has quickly become a second home to me. The people, the parks, the food are all divine. There's no place quite like it in all the world." He says it without sarcasm, but that almost makes it sound like a carefully packaged lie.

"Are you being honest now, or were you honest before?"

"Does it matter?"

If this is the direction my afternoon is headed, then I want off this train. *Be brave, Maddie. Just jump.* "Look, I *don't* want you to lie to me. If you can't say something nice or interesting or smart, then we'll rely on your good looks to carry your social media presence." Heck, while I'm off the rails, I might as well keep rolling. "I get that you don't want to be here, that you're hungry and probably tired after training. But I agreed not to film you with the kids, and I don't want to fail on my first intern assignment. I'd really appreciate it if you could be a professional for a few more minutes."

His mouth is open in shock, but his lips are curved up at the edges. Amused shock? Is that a thing? I'm weirdly pleased that I've managed to draw this sort of reaction.

"I'm sure," he says, tilting his head toward me, "I can find something interesting to say."

I circle my hand, urging him to do it.

"I do like Chicago. The city has a lot to offer, but . . ." He pauses, scooping up a bit of bread and cheese. "But I don't know that it will ever feel like home."

The silence stretches for a moment as I consider his words, his tone. There at the end, he sounded a little vulnerable, like he was actually divulging a truth. It may not have been the most flattering response, but the honesty and pinch of homesickness made it relatable.

"Okay." I nod slowly. "I think we can use that. What about—"

"No more questions until we eat something. Please." He waves to his food and says, "In Italy, we eat what's presented to us and then discuss business between courses."

That might be etiquette, but it feels like stalling. Still, I follow his lead to be polite, scooping the meat and cheese onto the bread but avoiding the eggplant.

"Are you from Chicago?" he asks as he creates his next bite.

"Is that an official question, or are you just making conversation?" I throw his words back at him.

His hand stops halfway to his mouth, and he flashes a smirk that I've seen in the tabloids. It's formulated for maximum devastation: teasing, naughty, completely effective. If this were a date, I'd puddle at his feet.

"I already told you we weren't discussing business."

"Oh, so casual conversation is allowed *while* we eat?"

The smirk melts into something more sincere, and strangely, it has a more potent impact on my insides. "Yes, of course. And?"

"And . . ." I shake off the feeling that's gooier than the melted mozzarella pictured on the menu. "Am I from Chicago? No. I'm from Normal. It's a few hours southwest of the city."

"Normal is a strange name."

"It's accurate."

"So Normal is . . ." He's done this before, pausing to search his vocabulary for the right term in English. "*Basic?*"

"Exactly!" I laugh. "It's your basic midwestern town."

The woman comes back with two small bowls full of steamy, creamy-looking rice speckled with mushrooms. She hurries away before I can thank her.

"How do you know the secret back doors to Chicago's best Italian restaurants?" I ask scooping some into my mouth. It tastes like comfort food, like something your mom made for you when you got a bad grade or someone was mean to you at school.

"Scott, actually. He studied abroad in Rome and came back to America dying to find the most authentic Italian food." He waves to our small enclosure. "And he found Maria and Moretti's."

"Ah. That's where he learned to speak Italian. Mystery solved."

"His Italian isn't *nearly* as good as he thinks it is." Gabe has two more spoonfuls of creamy rice in his bowl, but he pushes it to the side. I'm a little jealous he has any left. "Tell me more about yourself," he prompts.

"Why?"

"It's only fair that you should tell me about you, if you expect me to do the same. Besides, we'll be working together a lot, so—" he adds, making that pinching hand gesture Italians always do in movies, totally living up to the stereotype. I guess Italians really do talk with their hands. "I need to know who I'm in business with."

I remember the list hidden under the napkin on my lap. It's not that I forgot why I was here, but I sort of pushed it to the side of my mind. "Oh, I'm not that exciting. I'm just a normal girl from Normal." Wow. I couldn't have come up with anything to make me seem less boring? I hurry to add, "I mean, I'm working at Velocity so that I have something really compelling to put on my college application." I explain that I need a great letter of recommendation to boost my chances of getting into UNC.

"What do you have to do to succeed?"

Here's my opening. I prop my chin on my hands and try to look as innocent as possible. "Get you to answer these questions, for starters."

He sighs and shakes his head, but he's more amused than irritated. "We *are* between courses."

"Exactly." I look down at the list, trying to pick an easy question to start with, but they all seem a little intrusive. "I guess we'll start at the top. What is it about soccer that you love so much?"

"Calcio," he corrects, head canted like he's disciplining an unruly student. "I love calcio—that's 'soccer' in Italian."

"All right, fine. For the sake of this conversation, it's *calcio*." I tap the top of my straw, trapping a little water, then releasing it back into the cup. "What do you love about calcio?"

He leans back in the chair, seeming to consider my question, but since there isn't much space his leg slides all the way up my thigh. I jump at the sudden contact and nearly knock over my drink. Does he know his leg is against mine? Of course, he does. But is it on purpose? I mean, it's a small table. Surely, some leg brushing is acceptable. Pull it together, Mads.

"There is more . . . tension in calcio than any other sport. It's back and forth, fast and slow, give and take." He's focused on something over my shoulder, but I think he's watching a scene play out inside his head. "It builds and builds and builds before—" His eyes shift to me, pinning me in place.

I hold his stare but have to swallow before I can speak. "Before what?" My voice comes out a breathy whisper.

"Something breaks. There's a hole in the defense. A perfect pass. The ball sinks into the net." He tilts his head toward me, looking at me through his eyelashes. "Then ecstasy."

"*Ecstasy.*" I give a nervous-sounding laugh. "That's one word for it."

"Is it the wrong word? I mean . . ." He waves with his hand like he expects me to help him fill in the blank. "Everyone is relieved. The crowd cheers."

"Wow. Yeah. Relieved. Good description." I have a hard time formulating a follow-up question because my brain isn't functioning like it should be. I've never heard someone talk about a sport in such an intense way. "Is there anything else you're—umm—passionate about?"

He pushes his shoulder into the corner of the nook, letting it hold him up, and it alleviates the leg contact. "I play the piano a little."

"You have a grand piano in your apartment. Something about that makes me think you might play more than a little."

Gabe shrugs again. I've noticed it's a multifunctional gesture with any number of meanings—a yes, a no, a maybe.

"Does that mean you'd be willing to perform on camera?"

"Probably. My parents insisted that I be able to perform on command." Instead of being arrogant about this surprise talent, he seems reticent to talk about it. "They felt it was important that I had many skills."

"Being amazing at soccer wasn't enough?"

"It's never been enough."

There's something there, a curtain I want to peel back and peek behind. Not necessarily for the public but for myself. "What does that mean?"

The shutters drop on his expression. He takes a big breath, and I prepare myself to hear another nonanswer, but it never comes. A different woman, closer to our age but unquestionably related to Maria, brings two more plates of food. She lingers a little longer, eyeing me as she sets down a plate of what looks like chicken with roasted red peppers. Gabe says a couple sentences to her in Italian, and she tucks her hair behind her ear like she's flattered. I may not be able to translate what's being said, but body language makes me think they're flirting.

Because no one is immune to Gabriel Fortunato.

When she leaves, he motions to his food with his fork. "We're eating again, so it's your turn. What do you like to do?"

Nice redirection, but it does give me an opportunity to make up for my stupid answer about being normal. I tell him that I was a competitive dancer and taught classes until I came to Chicago.

"It sounds like you miss it."

I mimic his shrug. "Some parts. Getting ready for a performance. Being on stage. Seeing the littles I teach doing well."

"You must have been good."

I had moments when I knew I was, but dance wasn't something that came naturally. I had to work twice as hard as anyone else to learn a routine. Once my body built the muscle memory, I never forgot it, and performing was bliss. No one who watched me had any idea of the hours I stayed late just to keep up with my teammates, the sprained ankles and broken toes I danced on, or the sleep I lost trying to remember an eight count. Even though I loved it, the adrenaline rush, the way my body felt after practice, I knew it wasn't something I could do forever. Better to give it up before I broke something besides my heart.

"I was okay." I give a self-deprecating laugh. "*Not* good enough to perform on command."

"Too bad," he says, lifting a piece of perfectly cooked chicken to his mouth. "If I have to play the piano for you, then you should have to dance for me."

The line is delivered so smoothly that I almost don't notice that it's totally a *line*. The eyebrow tilt, the smirk, the pause before taking a bite. My brain screeches to a halt, my mental brakes squealing like my mom's Camry. Hold up. Gabriel Fortunato is flirting with *me*.

Or maybe being flirtatious is just his natural state?

Whether it is or not, I've been flirting back. Sort of unintentionally, sort of to manipulate answers out of him. The meat turns to ash in my mouth. I have to take a big gulp of water to wash the feeling away. "That's never going to happen," I finally answer.

"Why?" He seems honestly surprised. "If you're good, why don't you want to show off?"

"Because *I* don't have to show off to prove that I'm good."

"Ouch." He puts his hand over the middle of his chest. "That felt like it was directed at me. Are you saying I'm a show-off?"

"Are you saying that you're not?"

He laughs, and I can't help but smile at the way he takes my bullets—which I can't seem to stop firing. Ugh. I'm bantering. I should not be bantering with a client.

"You know my team has a charity banquet coming up?" He puts both forearms on the table and leans a little toward me. "There will be a dance floor. I think it's a perfect opportunity for you to prove you can dance."

"Hard pass."

He clicks his tongue. "I'll find some way to change your mind."

"Doubt it." I push away my unfinished plate, needing to veer away from this subject. "I just realized how late it's getting, and I really need to get back to Watford. He's been trapped in the apartment all day, and it has sort of become my responsibility to make sure he gets a walk. I hate to be impolite." Which is true. I really don't want to be rude, but we're at a private table and I'm having a hard time determining where the lines are. "Can I ask a few more questions, speed-round style? Then we can both get out of here because I'm sure you've got better things to do than hang out with me."

I'm totally doing the nervous fast-talking thing, and something about the wrinkle between his eyebrows makes me think he's noticed.

"Not really, but if you're in a hurry——"

"I am." *I am also so ridiculous.* "I would hate for Watty to make a mess."

"Of course," he says, breaking eye contact. "I understand."

I'm not even sure I understand it.

By the time Maria serves dessert, Gabe is giving me the shortest answers possible, and I stop asking the hard questions.

Me: Favorite color?

Him: Blue.

Me: Favorite animal?

Him: Dog.

Me: Favorite food?

Him: Italian. Is that even a question?

I have enough to work with, so I give up on the list and offer to pay for dinner—which would have to go on my dad's credit card. Gabe won't let me pay. I don't know what he says to Maria, but she seems shocked when he asks for the ticket, looking between us and at the barely touched tiramisu on my plate like that's an explanation.

"Everything was delicious," I say quickly. "It was the best dinner I've ever had. Especially the creamy rice."

"The risotto?" She smiles, but it seems a little trembly around the edges. "Come back and see us again?"

"Yes!" I stand up from the table, shaking the crumbs from my dress. "And I'll bring my aunt. She'll love it."

"Great. I'll look forward to it." She shakes my hand, which saves me from trying to figure out the Italian cheek-kissing thing and being afraid to turn my face the wrong way.

She says something in speedy Italian to Gabe, and I'm not sure what he says to her, but it sounds like reassurances. I start to sneak away, but Gabe notices, gives Maria two more cheek kisses, and hurries after me.

"You don't have to leave." I thumb toward Lincoln Park. "I'm only a few blocks from home. I can walk from here."

"If you're in such a rush, wouldn't it be faster if I drove you?" It's the polite thing to say, but it feels like he's checking my story.

"Don't feel obligated."

"I don't."

Could you maybe tell your face that, then? He's gone all steel-eyed and flat-mouthed, probably in response to me shifting from friendly to business. But it needed to be done. I slipped into the wrong head space, which involved analyzing every lip curl and arm brush, and had to get back to the right one.

"Fine. Sure. Thanks." I drop into the Ferrari, only speaking to give him directions to the Belden-Stratford. He answers with nods and *mm-hmm*s. When we pull under the awning, Doorman Kevin hurries down the stairs to open my side door.

"Miss Maddie!" He greets me with his booming baritone. "Are you and your *friend* here to stay?"

"No, he's just dropping me off." I swing my feet out of the car, then lean down so I can see Gabe's face. "Thanks for dinner. It was really nice."

"I'll be sure to pass your compliments to Maria." He slips on those mirrored glasses, and I swear it's like putting a physical wall between us.

"Later this week, we'll get video of you playing the piano?"

"If you must."

"I really, really must."

He nods, and I guess that passes for a goodbye, so I back away and let Kevin shut the door.

Gabe speeds out of the driveway faster than necessary, and I don't blame him. I sometimes wish I could run away from me too.

Thirteen

I WALK PAST LINCOLN PARK ZOO ON THE WAY TO WORK IN THE mornings. The big male lion has a routine where he roars over and over as the sun rises; I think that's how he lets his caretakers know he's hungry. The cows moo, begging to be milked. And the monkeys act like, well, monkeys. So, when I say the office is a zoo on Thursday, I'm speaking with some authority.

The exec that Javi works for created a portfolio weeks ago, got it proofread by the in-house technical writers and laid out by the design team, and okayed proofs from the printer. But as he flipped through the final copies this morning, he realized it was missing two key pages from the middle and two other pages were printed upside down. The printer they use is in Indiana and couldn't get new ones shipped to us before his presentation tomorrow.

So for the first time in the whole two weeks I've worked at Velocity, all five interns have been assigned to ditch their work and help Javi pull the project together. We run every copy machine and printer, collate, punch, and bind more than four hundred portfolios with nearly a hundred pages each. Katie's the official runner, grabbing copies off the machines, bringing us lunch and drinks.

At first, Mara tries to act like I don't exist, but by seven thirty in the evening, we've reached that stage of exhaustion where holding grudges requires too much energy. My shoes have been under the table for at least four hours, Arman is wearing his tie like a sweatband, Javi put his phone in a cup from the kitchen to amplify his running playlist so we can all work to the music, and Mara is singing along, at full volume. And that's when I realize that I like all of these people. They're smart, talented, and to varying degrees, funny. Javi is over-the-top hysterical, but Mara's snapbacks are wicked in the best ways. Arman is quiet, to match his voice, but he's steady and consistent. Katie is the perfect cheerleader, though I have a feeling that if I told her that, she'd be offended.

Best of all, I haven't thought about Gabriel Fortunato in at least twelve hours. Okay, fine. I've *thought* about him, but I haven't gotten a stomachache angsting over the way I acted yesterday. The farther I get away from that quiet little nook, the ambience of the kitchen, the closeness of our bodies, I realize it was all a *formula* for something romantic. Of course, it felt like flirting.

Hello, Self? You described yourself as normal. There were no sparks. If his leg bumped against yours, it wasn't flirtation. It was proximity. He's six two. You're five ten. It's not as if that space was designed for people with longer-than-average limbs.

"And that, ladies and gentlemen, is four hundred!" Javi does a running man. Arman joins in with a head-nodding groove. Katie shimmies, and Mara high-fives me.

I repeat: Mara high-fives *me*.

Today could totally have sucked, but instead, fences have been mended and baby seeds of friendship have been planted. I don't even care if it's trite, because it's true.

We all leave the building together, and this time I'm not excluded from the dinner invitation.

FRIDAY MORNING IS BACK TO BUSINESS AS USUAL, AND IT'S A TOTAL throat punch. I sit down at the front desk, ready to balance Patty's regular tasks and my assignments for the Fortunato account. But when I open the editing program, I can't find my folder anywhere. It's not just the last video I was working on that's missing, it's all four of them.

There has to be a logical explanation.

When William comes in, I snag him before he can slip through the secret door. "Hey! You didn't by chance move my video folder, did you?"

He's drinking a coffee from the booth on the first floor, but his eyebrows smash together as he swallows. "No. Did it get put into the general folder?"

"I didn't think to check there." I force a relieved smile to my face, but my heart is still fluttering like hummingbird wings.

"Emma told me what you'd done was great and said to let you play with the footage I shot too." He leans into the door, moving on to his next assignment. "I uploaded it to your folder on Wednesday."

There's nothing in my folder. I can't even find my folder. "Cool. I'll see what I can do with it." *Once I figure out where it went.*

Between calls and ushering a few clients to the executive offices, I explore every nook and cranny of the server. I search under Gabe's name, my name, Emma's, William's. I comb through every footage folder. I get locked out of the system for thirty minutes because I enter my password wrong three times because I'm typing too fast.

Katie and Mara come out the secret door at eleven, heading to lunch because it's Friday and we get to leave early.

"Send the phones to voice mail for ten and come down with us?" When Katie's cheerfulness fails to reach me, she leans across the top of the desk. "Everything okay?"

"I can't find the videos I was working on."

Mara copies Katie's stance, leaning over the high receptionist desk to look at my computer. "Didn't you back them up?"

"I didn't think I'd have to. Everything is sent to the server."

"That happened to me last year. The server eats things sometimes," she says, giving me a lopsided frown. "Back up everything in at least two places."

"It's not just one file, though. It's the whole folder." I run my hand through my hair, wishing for a tie to keep.

"Do you think someone deleted it on accident?" Katie asks, face concerned.

"No . . ." Well, I didn't. The only way to delete a whole folder is to drag it to the trash. I check the little garbage icon, and there's nothing there. Not even any of the early drafts of my edits that I deleted while I was working on Patty's computer. Someone emptied that too. Someone who had access to this desk.

"We better run, so we can get back." Mara's digging through her purse, not looking at me. Not making eye contact at all.

Katie doesn't say anything, but her forehead is wrinkled with worry.

"You guys go. I'm going to keep looking."

"Do you want anything?" Katie offers.

"No. I'll eat after I find the folder."

Mara finishes with her ChapStick and gives me a smile that falls a mile short of kind. "Sucks that this happened. I guess you'll know better for next time."

She wouldn't have deleted the files. That's just so low. She couldn't have possibly done that and then treated me so nicely yesterday. Could she? The accusation stays trapped behind my teeth, and I hold it there until they get into the elevator.

Even if Mara trashed all the videos—and I don't want to believe that she did—it doesn't change the fact they're gone.

I ring William's office from the front desk.

"Hey! Quick question." I try to sound cheery instead of shaken. "You don't by chance have the footage still on your phone, do you?"

"Nope. I deleted them once they were on the server. They take up too much space on my phone."

Oh no. "I can't seem to find them."

He lets out a deep, frustrated-sounding breath. "Well, I don't know what to tell you. Look again."

And I do. But they aren't there.

They aren't anywhere.

My family has this old laptop that gets really hot when you use it. The fan inside whirs around and around and around until the laptop finally overheats and shuts down. I totally get how the poor little machine feels.

Even though I hate to admit it to myself, I screw up little things all the time, despite my best efforts. I can't count the number of times I've stayed up late working on a project, only to leave it on the kitchen table. Or pack my dance bag the night before practice but leave my shoes on the floor beside it. Luckily, my mom works from home and has always been able to bail me out.

Who's going to rescue me when I'm at UNC and leave my home-work/laptop/brain in my apartment?

Just one more reason my parents don't think it's worth the money for me to go somewhere far from home.

I've got to figure out how to get my crap together.

I systematically click through every accessible file that's been created in the past two weeks, just in case. Not there. It's not on the front desk's computer. It's not on my laptop either. I've never had a panic attack, but the pounding in my chest and the swirling in my head make me think I'm close to having my first.

What am I going to do? What can I do?

I grab my phone and call my brother.

"Is this a butt dial?" he asks, sounding both surprised and happy.

"If someone deleted a file, is there a way to get it back?"

"I'm doing great. Thanks for asking." He has a laugh in his voice, and it's not helping.

"Max, I love you. But I'm panicking here." I keep my voice just over a whisper, terrified someone will hear me and report back to the management. "I don't have time to joke about this."

"What happened?"

I explain everything as fast as I can, which is pretty fast because sometimes I speak at Mach speeds. Luckily, Max is used to me.

"Are you saying she sabotaged you?"

"Not the point of this conversation."

He sighs. "Right, we'll get back to that later. I can send you a link for some directions that might bring your files back, but it's been more than twenty-four hours. There's a good chance that an in-house server clears the system."

I lean my forehead against the edge of my desk, trying to get my breathing under control. "Okay."

"But if it doesn't work—and I'm not saying that's going to happen—did you think about calling Fortunato and asking to film him again?"

No, I didn't. Because that sounds like a horrible idea. "I'd have to tell Emma and William that the files got deleted, and that would mean I screwed up." *Again.*

"So, don't tell them. Just call Fortunato and tell him you need more footage ASAP. If he's in such big trouble and really wants to turn things around, he'll do it without question."

When I don't answer immediately, Max adds, "Mads, just ask nicely. Tell him that the files got deleted and you're going to be in huge trouble if you don't get the footage. If he's anything like me, he'll jump at the chance of being a hero."

"He's nothing like you."

Max blows a frustrated raspberry. "Fine. Don't do it. Fess up, or better yet, tell Emma that you think this Mara girl deleted the files."

"Is there any way to prove it?" I sound whiny to my own ears.

"On a system where everyone has access? That's a negative, Ghost Rider."

"Ugh. No more *Top Gun.*"

"You're welcome." His sarcasm carries through the phone, and I can imagine him kicked back in the desk chair in his bedroom.

I almost smile, which makes me realize my heart rate has slowed a little. "Sorry. Thank you."

"Did Mom tell you we're coming down for the Fourth of July?"

My hackles rise, and angry goose bumps break out along my arms. "Coming to check on me, you mean?"

He gives his pity laugh. I recognize it because it's the male version of my own. "I'm sure that's her real motive, but I think she's couching it as a last family vacation."

The words are like stepping on one of Cube's Legos—a completely unexpected, sharp pain. "Oh, that's so sad." And it is. Max is more than ready for college, but that doesn't mean it's going to be easy to let him go. "Who's going to sit on the end of my bed and talk me down when I do something ridiculous?"

"You *can* call me, you know."

"You'll be too busy for me."

He's silent for too long. "Probably."

I laugh at his honesty, which is also so Max. "I hate you."

"Feeling's mutual, but even so I'm trying to convince Mom to let you come out and visit me before Christmas."

"Really? That would be— Crap. That's the elevator. Got to go." I hang up before he says anything else, but almost instantly, the link he promised pops up on my phone. I don't tell him very often, but he's the best.

The elevator doors slide open, and Katie and Mara spill out, laughing about something. They each have bags from the salad place up the street, but Katie sets a cookie and a scrunchie on my desk as she walks by with a wink.

For a moment, I'm stunned by her kindness. She knew exactly what I needed and followed through. Her thoughtfulness has a calming effect on my panic.

I throw my hair up in a ponytail, then follow the directions from Max's link. I didn't even know a History button existed, but there are William's videos. Hallelujah.

One small problem: There's still no sign of mine.

OR FUTURE REFERENCE, HITTING THE REFRESH BUTTON OVER and over doesn't actually change the files in your history folder. Neither does shutting down your computer and restarting it. Or crying onto your keyboard.

I don't actually cry, but I know all about the stages of grief thanks to my psychology class and I process through them in a hurry.

Denial: The files are not gone. They're here somewhere. I know it.

Anger: How could this possibly have happened?

Bargaining: If I just unplug you, will you bring my files back?

Depression: Noooooooooo!

Acceptance: Okay, the files are gone. What do I do about it?

I fix the problem, that's what.

At twelve thirty, after most of the floor has cleared out for the weekend, I peek into Emma's office. The space is a glass cube filled with white-and-silver furniture in sleek, futuristic lines. Like her apartment, it's a reflection of another side of her personality—efficient and functional while maintaining an air of quality and class. I tap on the all-glass door, totally different from the wood doors that front the junior executives' offices, and she waves me in without looking up from whatever she's working on.

Watford lifts his head, sees that it's me, and rolls onto his side.

Emma greets me with more enthusiasm than the dog. "Yesterday was so crazy that I forgot to ask how your meeting with Gabe went."

I lay it out for her, ending with getting my questions answered at Moretti's.

"Maddie! This is fabulous." She slaps her desk with excitement. "I had no idea he was multitalented."

"Yeah." I have to swallow before I lie. My mom has a magical sense about when I'm not being one hundred percent honest, but I'm hoping it's another thing that doesn't extend to Emma. "I thought I'd get some video of him playing the piano and doing a few other things." Like everything I lost, which is sad because the fast footwork video was so good.

"Great. Go ahead and set it up with him."

Do not collapse. Do not show relief. "Okay, sure. Do you think I need to get William to go with me or—"

"No, he's buried in survey analysis. Can you handle Gabe by yourself?"

"I totally can!" *Chill a bit, Mads. Don't give it away now.* "I mean, I just think this is a great opportunity to show William that I'm really good at this job."

"Agreed."

I'm texting Gabe before I'm all the way down the hall.

Me: Hi. I'd like to iron out a time to meet and get some other clips filmed for your social media accounts. Specifically, you playing the piano. Please let me know what times will be suitable. But as soon as possible. Please.

Instantly, my phone buzzes.

Gabe: You said please twice.

I can totally imagine the snotty tone of his voice. I manage not to respond with an eyeroll emoji, even though that's exactly what I do physically.

Me: Sorry.

Gabe: Now you have a 1-word response?

My expression morphs into an unwilling smirk.

Me: Maybe.

Gabe: Yes.

Fine. I can play this game with you.

Me: ???

Gabe: Sunday.

I send him a pin emoji because that requires no words but conveys my need for a location perfectly. Top that, sucker. He responds with a pinned address, which, depending on the rules of this particular game, is on par with my text. Then I realize that I'm playing with freaking Gabriel Fortunato instead of simply getting the job done.

Me: What time?

Gabe: 7 p.m.

Me: It might take a while.

He sends an "okay" emoji. I hate him because he's winning.

I walk back to Aunt Em's office to let her know my plan, but she's on the phone. Her elbow is on her desk, forehead in her palm, crumpled tissue on the calendar in front of her. It's shocking to see her so upset. Even when my grandpa died, she managed to laugh and tell jokes and reminisce about the good times with her father. She spoke so eloquently at his funeral that I wished I would have known Papa better, and Em didn't shed a single tear. What could shake her so badly now?

Watford rises from his spot beneath her desk and puts his paw on her arm; he senses something is wrong.

I want to do the same, but when she pushes him away, I know she's not in the mood to be bothered. Instead of waiting for her call to end, hovering outside the glass office like a creeper, I borrow a ring-light tripod from the storage room, put my company-issued laptop into my bag since I'm going to need it over the weekend, and clean off Patty's desk.

When I check back in, Emma's typing on her computer with her back to her office door.

"I'm ready to head out," I whisper, opening the door just wide enough to stick my head through. "Are you going to be leaving soon?"

She turns around to face me, and it's as if nothing happened. No puffy eyes or streaked makeup. No remnant of her breakdown a few minutes before.

"Not yet. I've got a couple things to do, but do you mind taking Watford?"

"Sure."

He's curled around her feet, and when she pulls out his harness, he refuses to stand up. "Come on, Watty." He usually lifts one paw to make it easier to slip his leg through the hole, but he grunts and curls up tighter.

Emma shakes her head, amused. "Doesn't my big baby want to go on a walk?" she says in her stupid dog-voice. He licks her hand, then puts his nose against her ankle. "I have no idea why he's being so clingy."

I do. Watford might be big and drooly, but he's also smart. She scrubs his ears tenderly. "I guess I'll bring him when I come home."

"Sounds good. Do you need anything?" *Like someone to talk to.* I don't say that, but I wonder if she might need someone to listen.

"Are we still on for steak frites?" she asks.

"Yep."

"Then we don't need anything else."

I stop at the convenience store anyway and pick up a half gallon of mint chocolate chip ice cream—Em's favorite.

I have a feeling we'll both need it before this weekend is over.

I'M CURLED UP ON THE COUCH EDITING WILLIAM'S FOOTAGE BY THE time Emma gets home at a little after five.

"Hi," she says on an exhale, kicks off her nude sling-backs by the door, and sweeps my feet off the couch.

"You okay?" I ask, as she plops down beside me.

Watford tries to climb into the space between us, but there really isn't enough room. His head is on Emma's leg; his butt is on me. Neither of us move to push him away even though he's smelly from his walk home.

"Do you care if we order up?" she asks. "We can still have steak frites, but wouldn't it be better to eat in our pajamas?"

Nice deflection, Em. "Sounds great to me." Especially since I'm already in my jams.

She makes the call, and I go back to editing. William's footage is not as good as mine, so making it look decent isn't nearly as easy as it was when I was working on my own. He filmed everything at eye level, which is fine for candid things but means I can't replicate anything I'd already done.

Emma comes out of her bedroom, face scrubbed, hair tied on top of her head. With her sloppy clothes on, she looks younger. Not that thirty-eight is ancient, but without her fancy wardrobe and perfect appearance, she seems more than six years younger than my mom.

She turns on a recorded episode of *The Bachelorette*, and we eat in front of the TV in near silence. This is not normal.

"Em, did something happen today? You seem off."

She takes a long time chewing and swallowing one of her blue cheese–sprinkled fries. "Geoff called."

It takes me a moment to process the name. He stopped being Uncle Geoff before the divorce was even final; I haven't thought about him with that moniker since the last Christmas they spent with my family. They could have stayed in any hotel, but they always wanted to be part of the Christmas morning experience. Cube was so infatuated with the magic of Santa Claus, and watching him open presents was adorable. Every year Mom bought Em and Geoff plaid pajama pants to match ours, and they sat in the recliner together, whispering about when they'd have kids of their own and the traditions they'd carry on. That last Christmas wasn't any different than any of the five previous years—except we had more snow than usual, and Geoff helped us build a tunnel the entire length of our backyard.

None of us knew at the time that he was already hooking up with the Olympian. None of us knew that he was the biggest fake that ever existed.

"You mean The Cheating Bastard?"

She cringes like she'd just bit her tongue. "You've really got to stop calling him that."

"Doesn't make it untrue." Doesn't change the sour taste I get in my mouth every time I think about him. Doesn't change that he hurt my aunt. Doesn't change the fact that so many of my Christmas memories, my first trip to New York, and my *only* trip to the ocean are tainted by his presence.

"I don't want to say 'You'll understand when you get older' because I hope you never do." She closes her eyes and rests her head against the back of the couch. "Relationships are complicated. Even when someone breaks your heart, even after they hurt you, it's hard to stop loving them."

I don't want to say that I understand because, even though Geoff betrayed our family, his actions absolutely gutted Emma. Today might have been the first time I'd seen Emma cry, but it wasn't the first time I'd *heard* her. She came to live with us for a few months while the divorce was being finalized and their home was being sold. In front of us, she was fine, Super-Fun Aunt Em, but at night, I could hear her sob-filled conversations with my mom. She blamed herself for his affair, saying that she hadn't spent enough time being present, being there when he needed her. She said she was too wrapped up in the business of being his wife, instead of loving him like she should have.

To me, it was all just a weird sort of justification. Geoff made a bad decision, and no matter what Emma did or did not do, she couldn't control his actions. He was a big boy, and he'd made the decision to cheat.

The thing is, I know Geoff loved Emma. I know it like I know my parents love each other. What I can't understand is choosing, over and over, to put yourself in a position to hurt someone you love.

Before I can talk again, I have to do some chewing of my own. "What did Geoff have to say?"

She sighs and nibbles the end of a fry. "He'll be in town next week, and he wants to see Watford."

"Which means he'll have to see you."

Nodding, miserable, Emma picks through her frites until she finds another piece of blue cheese.

"And you still love him."

She shrugs. "I shouldn't."

But that doesn't mean she doesn't. I'm not really sure what to do with that revelation. There's a part of me that wants to offer to take Watford to wherever they're meeting and give Geoff a piece of my mind. And there's a part of me—the little girl part who remembers riding on his shoulders and wearing his jersey—who wishes things could go back to the way they were before.

Except I know there's never any going back.

My voice is small. "I got ice cream even though you told me not to."

Emma's face breaks into its widest smile. "Let's bust that out."

There's no resolution to our conversation, no clear decision made or plans laid, but we sit close to each other, eating ice cream out of the same container, and we're okay.

I TRY TO BE SLY ON SUNDAY AFTERNOON AND SEND GABE THIS text:

Me: I borrowed a light and a tripod from Velocity. See you at 7!

I wanted to remind him that we had plans without making him feel like he needed to be reminded.

Gabe: Did you want me to pick you up?

Yes, my brain supplies. The equipment is really heavy, especially when you're trying to lug it on the bus. But I don't say that.

Me: That's not necessary. No need to go out of your way.

Gabe: I'll meet you outside your place at 7.

I take far too long getting ready and can't decide if I should wear something out of Emma's closet or something that I packed. I don't want to look like I'm trying too hard to be professional or sexy. I want to hit that narrow gap between *I always dress like this* and *I always look good*. Finally, I decide on a black cold-shoulder blouse of Em's and a pair of white shorts.

And then I sit on the front porch of the Belden-Stratford for twenty minutes.

"It's probably just traffic," Doorman Kevin says, checking his watch too. "Did you text him?"

"I am now."

I wait twenty more minutes, then gather my bags off the front stairs.

Kevin gives me a tight-lipped frown. "He'll have a good excuse."

Not to return my text or answer any of my calls? Doubtful. "Let's hope, Kevin."

He holds open the gold-framed glass door so I can slide through, feeling more than the weight of the bags dragging me down. I ignore Jan's closed-lipped smile and hold my key-pass toward the electronic lock.

"Madeline!"

I turn to find Gabe half jogging across the lobby toward me. "I'm sorry I was late." He whisks the bag out of my hand. "Let's get going."

A part of me wants to let him walk away, but I'm at his mercy for the footage. I'm not going to let my anger—and slightly injured feelings—stand in the way of doing my job, so I trail him out of the building. He's a troubled soccer star; I'm an intern. I shouldn't be surprised he doesn't value my time.

Not that it bothers me any less.

Kevin is waiting by the still-running Ferrari, expression shifting to relief when Gabe and I trot back.

"Good luck, Miss," he says as I climb in the car.

I don't know why I need luck, but I say thanks anyway.

Leaning against the car door, I look out the passenger window as Gabe pulls out of the Belden-Stratford. He drives with one hand, tapping his thumb against the steering wheel to some unheard beat.

Eventually, he clears his throat. "Are you going to ask me why I was late?"

I want to, but I won't. "Nope."

"Are you doing the one-word thing again?"

"No." I mean, I just did, but it wasn't intentional.

He chuckles softly. "You seem upset. Are you mad at me?"

"I'm not." There. Two words. And a total lie. Of course, I'm mad. I waited for him for an hour, and he didn't bother to call. But it's more than just being late. I know my job is to help him develop a public persona, but I'm not sure when he's being real and when he's camera ready. Is he the grouchy hoodie-wearing soccer star or the flirty guy from Moretti's?

"I don't believe you," he says.

I use his shrug. Let him translate that.

Neither of us speak until we're crossing the Chicago River. He clears his throat. "Did you know Chicago is haunted?"

"What?" I turn toward him, face scrunching at this sudden, random piece of information.

"Most of the old European cities are too, but I didn't know Chicago had as much history."

"You mean from the Chicago Fire?"

"Not only that. There are a lot more stories that I learned about on a Ghost Tour—"

"On a *what?*"

I didn't think it was possible for Gabriel Fortunato to blush. His shoulders lift toward his ears in a sheepish shrug. "I like history and I was bored last night. They had tickets available."

"Wait. You went on a Ghost Tour *last night?* Is that why you were late today?" I completely ignore the information about him being bored. Surely, he could find someone to hang out with. "Because you spent all night hunting ghosts?"

"No." He shakes his head once. "I was late because my sister had my car."

"Your sister?"

"Yeah. Iliana? You met her at my apartment the other day? She made you coffee."

"That was your *sister*?" The woman at his apartment looked nothing like the little girl in the picture in his file. Puberty was kind to someone.

"Wait . . ." A hint of humor bleeds into his voice. "Who did you think she was?"

"It doesn't matter." If I blow by this subject, I won't have to explain that I thought Bar Girl was a girlfriend or hookup or something else. "Was your phone dead or broken or lost? Or did you lose my number? Or—"

"Dio, stop! I'm sorry, okay? Iliana came home later than she was supposed to, and we argued, and I forgot my phone and didn't have the address, so I had to drive over to Moretti's so that I could try to remember which hotel you lived in."

"You couldn't have just typed in 'hotels near Lincoln Park Zoo?'" I lean over and tap on the GPS installed in the console. Four options come up. "Oh."

"I wasn't sure which one it was." His voice is contrite, and both his hands clench the steering wheel. "I really was trying to get there on time. Everything seemed to work against me today."

In other words, he had a day similar to so many of mine. No matter how much I've prepped, how much I've tried to do all the right things, something always goes wrong. Which is why I'm in this car in the first place. Despite my very best efforts, the universe is always working against me.

The silence is thick enough to slice into pieces and eat alongside my guilt. "Sorry I accused you of sleeping all day," I say softly.

"Fa niente." He punctuates the phrase with another shrug.

A part of me wants to hit him in his stupid shoulder so he can't use it to communicate. "I have no idea with that means."

"It's like . . . no problem. Don't worry."

"Fa niente?" I repeat, letting the last syllable float up like a question.

He nods, grin going crooked. "Good."

He opened the conversational door, and now it's my job to keep it open. I bite my bottom lip as I try to come up with something easy. "Did you think of anything to play tonight?"

Gabe raises his eyebrows at me, giving me that rakish smirk. "It's a surprise."

His apartment is pitch black when he unlocks the door. The drapes on the windows overlooking Navy Pier and the lake are shut tight. He fumbles for the light switch on the wall, which turns on two dim lamps on side tables. I guess the lighting is supposed to be moody, but mostly, it's just dark.

He drops my equipment bag on his sofa and starts opening the curtains. There's a thumbnail of sunlight reflecting over the waves, but the Ferris wheel is already lit, casting bright beams of light onto the water on either side of the pier. I don't even want to know how much he pays for this view, but we're going to get some use out of it today.

"Oh, this is perfect." I don't bother with the tripod. "Sit down. Play something while the light is so good."

"Already?"

"Yes!" I ignore the way his voice pitches a little high. "Go."

I set myself up in the piano's curve, leaning awkwardly over the top to get his face and hands in the shot. It's not very often that I'm grateful for my height, but today, it's an advantage.

He sits on the bench, rubs his palms against his thighs a couple of times, and places his hands on the keyboard. He looks up at me, waiting for my cue to start. I push the button, wait two seconds, and mouth, "Go."

His right hand starts first, slowly, just thumb and pinky hitting the keys. Then, the left hand drops in, and goose bumps shoot up my arms. His fingers dance over the keys, body rocking naturally with the rhythm. I know this song; it was my competition solo last year, but I've never heard it played like this. It's intricate and delicate, but that doesn't take the power from it.

He looks up from the keyboard, meeting my gaze, and his attention is like a touch—a fingertip tracing my collarbone or the brush of lips on the back of my neck. When his eyes return to the keys, I take an unsteady breath.

I never imagined that watching him play the piano would be so personal. He finishes the song, holding a deep bass note until it fades away, and I stop recording.

"Well . . ." I pause, trying to shake off the music's hold. "I guess you aren't just arrogant. You're actually *that* good."

Gabe gives a surprised half laugh. "Thank you, I think?"

"You're welcome." Pressing into the piano's side, elbows on the lip, I click the video to watch the playback. Gabe stands up from the bench and steps behind me, watching over my shoulder. His presence is warm, his breath fluttering my hair. My eyes are on the screen, but every inch of my body is focused on him. His denim-clad leg is brushing my knee. His right arm has me half-caged against the piano.

I've dated a little. I've kissed a lot. But never in any of those hurried moments on my doorstep or in someone's basement have I been so aware of another person.

The video ends. I'm afraid to turn around, to look up from my phone. I swallow to force some moisture into my mouth. "So?" I manage, rewinding the footage, to that moment when he looked at me over the piano. My heart trips in my chest and tumbles down my rib cage, knocking into each bone along the way. "What do you think?"

He drops back onto the piano bench with a thump. "I hate it."

"What? Why?"

Gabe's head is down, and he trails his fingers over an angry-sounding minor key. "Shoot it from the other side."

"But the view of Navy Pier—"

"Is part of the problem. There are people out there who will try to pinpoint which apartment building I'm in, and then wait for me to come down." He looks up but only makes eye contact for a second before turning back to the piano. "Or worse, they'll figure out how to get up here. I don't need that. Iliana doesn't either."

"That's not even possible. What are they going to do? Count the windows?"

"Maybe? It's happened before."

"People came to your *house?*"

He doesn't look at me, eyes focused on the keys. "In Italy, yes. And to my gym. And to my car. They threw rocks; cracked my windshield." He swallows and then looks up at me. "Did you hear about the fan that tried to attack me during a training session in Barcelona?"

I come around the piano and sit beside him on the bench. "No."

"I'm not surprised." His laugh is cold. "The cameras cut away when fans get on the field. Don't want to encourage other people to try."

"He got onto the field?" Every time he answers a question, the knot in my throat grows exponentially.

Gabe runs his fingers through his hair. "Past security, over the barricades. If it wasn't for my teammates . . ."

"They stopped him?"

"Yeah." A ghost of a smile drifts onto his face. "You don't mess with my teammates."

My shoulders round with realization. "This is why there's nothing personal on any of your accounts."

"Partially. I just—" He cuts off, playing a harsh melody. "Everyone *hated* me after the World Cup. There are probably people in Italy who always will. When everything that is personal—your successes, your failures, your most private moments—becomes public, those things don't belong to you anymore."

His words hit me like the flu. My stomach twists with nausea and my bones feel like they're jammed together too tightly. "We don't have to do this. If you want to keep this to yourself, then you should." Even if it leaves me nothing to work with.

His voice is soft when he speaks again. "I'm so tired of people judging everything I do and never finding me good enough. Can you imagine what kind of things people might say when they see this?"

His expression is so open, so vulnerable.

"They're going to see that you're so talented." I can't help but grab his hand.

He gives me a bashful smile, the one that's reserved for moments like this, and I realize that Gabriel Fortunato—world-famous soccer star—is nervous. He swallows, the knob of his throat rising and falling, and he takes a deep breath. He's visibly steeling himself. "I made you a promise. You agreed to not take pictures of the kids, and you didn't. Will this song be enough?"

My eyes drop to his mouth as he talks, and the words, the way his lips form around them, and it's almost enough to make me forget what question I'm answering. "Of course." I stand, needing to extract myself from the pull of Gabriel Fortunato. "But I will never push you into doing anything that doesn't feel right."

"Thank you." Gabe lets out a long, slow breath. "I can't remember the last time someone cared about how I felt."

My heart swells inside my chest, pressing against my lungs. I hurt for him, but I'm also a little angry. He's not Cube. He's not a little kid who got bullied on a playground, but the emotion that shoots through my veins is the same I feel on my brother's behalf. Gabe is older and bigger and probably more mature than me, but that doesn't mean he defends himself to the adults who are supposed to have his best interests at heart.

"I'll just grab my stuff and let you get back to your weekend."

"No, don't go." He moves over to the tripod bag and starts to pull out the equipment. "We'll close the drapes and you can film it from the other side."

"Really? I don't—"

"Really."

And I know he means it. He plays the song two more times, with the phone at different angles so I can splice the footage together later tonight. It will look professional, but it lacks the passion of the first recording. Which no one will ever notice because no one will know the other recording exists.

It's not *that* late, but I'm not brave enough to ask him to help me replace the lost footage after everything he's just said. I do, however, need his approval on the other videos and photos.

We set up at the kitchen bar, lights blazing, respectful distance between us, as I pull up the campaign and the elements on my laptop that will go live over the next two weeks.

"Didn't you get any footage from the training day?" he asks after I click through the edits I made to William's video. "You weren't just lying on the field for fun, right?"

I push him with my shoulder. "I actually got some great stuff, but . . ." I hesitate. Max said Gabe would want to be the hero, but asking for help is harder than I imagined. With a deep breath, I add, "But somehow everything I loaded to the server got deleted and my aunt *may* kill me for it."

"Can we replace it?" He stands up and snatches his workout bag from under the coffee table and pulls out a soccer ball. "There's a deck on top of the building with a putting green. Let's go up there and figure it out."

It's such a sweet offer. "I don't want to put you out."

"It's not," he says, already grabbing my gear bag. "It's almost dark. No one will be able to tell where we're at."

I bite the inside of my cheek, considering. "Are you sure?"

"I promised you something better. Let's go get it."

We go to the roof, which is sparsely decorated with a lounge set, fire pit, and a few planters with the putting turf off to one side. He dribbles, juggles, and runs himself through drills, while I film the whole thing—including him shooting the ball at the rooftop decor. He's ridiculously accurate.

I collapse onto the little strip of fake grass as I skim through the different clips. "This is going to be so good."

He drops down next to me, flat on his back, pillowing his head on his arms. "Of course it is."

The return of his confidence makes me smile.

"Are you coming to the team's charity gala? I heard they outsourced a lot of the work to Velocity."

I shrug, watching the playback. "If my aunt wants me to go, I guess I'll be there."

"What if I want you there?"

"I'm sure Em won't mind." I tilt my phone toward him. "You know what would be perfect to go along with this—"

He covers the screen, so I look at him, momentarily irritated. Then I notice that he's rolled onto his side, head propped on his hand, and anything sharp I'd planned to say gets soft around the edges.

"Come as my date?"

I'm painfully aware of his hand over mine, fingers skimming the inside of my wrist. Of the way his T-shirt snags against my hip every time he inhales. Of the hint of scruff on his chin.

"Why?" My voice is a breathless whisper. Everything about him is formulated to steal my good sense and ability to speak in sentences.

"We've had a good time together, right?" He moves the hand from my phone to my kneecap and gives it a playful shake. "Plus, someone from Velocity will have to be there anyway. If I get to pick, I'd choose you."

He says it in an offhanded way, but his proximity plus the hand on my knee makes me think that on some level he actually means it.

Gabriel Fortunato wants to take me on a date.

My body is screaming its approval, but my brain is a little slower. Is this a good idea? Is this against some rule system? Is this unprofessional? Do I care?

A group of people crash through the patio door, laughing loudly. Gabe is instantly on his feet. At first I think it's because he's moving away from me, but then I notice a familiar face among the partiers.

"Iliana?" Gabe says, crossing the space toward his sister.

Her eyes go wide and guilty. "I didn't think you'd be up here."

"What . . . why are they here?"

"Don't worry. They're my friends." She reaches up and pats his cheek with the slow deliberation of someone who has had far too much to drink, and judging from the way the others lean against each other and the walls, I think all of her friends are in the same state.

One of the guys tries to push past Gabe, but he shifts to block the pathway to the furniture.

"You need to go," Gabe says, voice low and full of threat.

The laughter stops. Iliana says something in fast Italian, hand gripping Gabe's chin. He shakes her off. "Don't make me call security."

"Come on, man. She invited us up here," the guy nearest the door whines.

"Get. Out."

Everyone sobers a little, and the guys retreat. The other girl lingers in the doorway, face undecided.

"You're blowing this way out of proportion. None of them even *care* who you are." Iliana takes a step away from him, but turns her ankle in her super-high stilettos and stumbles like a baby deer.

Gabe catches her around the waist, shooting me an embarrassed look. "I'll be back."

I feel sick. I'm not really sure what's going on, but none of it's good. And I think to minimize everyone's embarrassment, it'd be better if I just left.

Tossing the tripod and light back into its bag and tucking my laptop under my arm, I hurry to the elevator.

A taxi is idling in front of the building, and I jump inside, grateful I don't have to wait one more minute to get home. As I shut the door, I get a text message.

Gabe: If you would have waited, I would have driven you home.

I want to type: "Wait while you argue with your sister? Thanks, but no thanks." Awkward isn't a big enough word to describe how that would have made me feel.

Instead, I play it off. Autocorrect tries to change my response, but I finally get it to switch to Italian:

Me: Fa niente.

It's not a big deal to me, but I bet it's huge to him.

Sixteen

EMMA AND WILLIAM APPROVE THE VIDEOS FIRST THING MONDAY morning, and we debate whether or not to start with the piano footage or to wait until we're sure we've got the world's attention. Emma says watching Gabe play is remarkable, and William shakes his head in amazement. I pretend it's because of the way I edited it—splicing the angles together, playing with the filters—but I know it's because he's just that good.

Once the schedule is set, William shows me how to load everything into the automated system. The piano footage will post in thirty minutes, and we're hoping for eight thousand likes in the first hour. Emma says that will determine whether or not the video will go viral. Everyone on our staff has been notified to like and share from all their social media accounts the moment it drops. I send out positive vibes to the universe, hoping the rest of the world will do the same.

Part of my job will now involve tracking engagements and the hashtags that seem to work best, which means I have to spend at least a few hours every day looking at pictures of Gabriel Fortunato and remembering just how stupid I am.

Gabe dates models and actresses. He hangs out with rock stars and designers. Under no circumstances would he be interested in an *intern*. He only asked me to accompany him to the gala because I'm a better option than Emma or William.

"Hey!" Katie literally swings into my cubicle, hanging on to the door frame with one hand and leaning forward until her momentum spins her into my space. "How was your weekend?"

"Fine. Nothing exciting to report."

Katie's face crumples. "You don't look fine. You look tired."

She's not wrong. I'm exhausted. I stayed up way too late to edit the footage, and I didn't even bother to steal anything out of Emma's closet. I debate telling her everything—about Gabe and the hospital kids, and the piano playing, and the scene with his sister—but I don't. I haven't been sworn to secrecy, but it doesn't feel like my story to tell. So instead, I say, "I worked all weekend on Fortunato stuff. How was yours?"

She launches into a spiel about training for her triathlon and the cute guy from her training group and how hard it is to make transitions when your swimwear is wet. And by the end of it all, I feel better. Katie managed to pull some of the sunshine and the lake in with her, brightening my whole cubicle.

Then, William darkens my doorway, frowning at both of us before speaking. "Morning, Coffee. Intern." He nods toward the ugly conference room. "We're having an impromptu staff meeting regarding upcoming events."

Mara, Javi, and Arman are each looking at their phones when Katie and I walk into the room. From the music, I know they're watching the piano video.

"This is awesome, Maddie." Arman offers me a high five. "I never would have guessed he could play so well."

Javi agrees, sort of unwillingly, but Mara doesn't look up from her phone. She starts it again, while William writes on the whiteboard.

"Where was this filmed at?" she asks as I drop into the chair across from hers.

"At his apartment. He has a grand piano—"

"You were at his apartment over the weekend?" She gives me a smug smirk, then makes eye contact with Javi. "How . . . cozy."

"Can't blame her for mixing business with pleasure." Javi gives me a super-suggestive wink.

"It's not like that," I say. Even though what I'm saying is completely true, I can't lie to myself. My heart leaps every time my phone buzzes, or I see a picture of him, or I hear his name. And even though I know it's impossible, there's a part of me that wishes it *was* like Mara and Javi are assuming. "It was convenient."

"I bet it was." Mara is grinning like the Cheshire Cat, all malevolent and evil.

"Enough." William draws a big star next to "Fire Party." "At the end of the month, Velocity is helping with the Chicago Fire's annual charity banquet. Over the next couple weeks, you'll all be assigned to double-check RSVPs, personalize gift baskets for your attendees, and handle some sponsorship-related tasks."

My phone vibrates, and I steal a peek.

Gabe: What do you think of me cooking at Moretti's? It might be funny.

Me: Funny because you can't cook?

Gabe: There isn't anything I can't do.

It's such a Gabe response that I can't help but shake my head at the arrogance.

Me: So you can cook?

Gabe: I'm willing to learn, and Maria is willing to teach me tomorrow.

Gabe: I think it might help their business.

I'm pleasantly surprised that he's thinking of social media ideas on his own and that he wants to do something that will benefit someone else.

Me: I thought you wanted to keep Moretti's a secret?

Gabe: I can always come in through the back door.

Me: The video is up. Did you see it?

"Coffee?" William has an Expo marker pinched between his fingers, face equally pinched. Everyone around the table is staring at me, waiting for me to respond to the question my brain didn't register. "Did you hear anything I said?"

I drop my phone into my lap. "Sorry. What?"

Mara rolls her eyes. Because that's way more professional than me on my phone in a meeting.

William releases an irritated-sounding breath but presses on without saying anything about my lack of focus. "It's a red-carpet event, so we'll need all of you that night. You'll circulate through the crowd, make sure our clients are taken care of, and help out wherever you might be needed."

Katie waves one hand to get William's attention. "Will we get to dress up, or are we like waitstaff?"

"It's formal, Intern. You will need to be dressed appropriately."

"Sweet." Javi gives a little shoulder shimmy. "I look amazing in a tux."

We all laugh, even Mara.

William gives us all assignments—while I covertly steal peeks at the rising total of likes, holding my breath every time it jumps by double or triple digits.

"I think that about covers it. Get back to work." William starts to erase his calendar. "Except you, Coffee."

Crap. I'm definitely in trouble. And it could totally be my imagination, but I swear Mara is thrilled about it as she bounces out of the conference room. And I'd just gotten used to her stomping around the office.

Once everyone is gone, I say, "I was texting Gabe—er, Fortunato—during the meeting. He wants to set up a shoot at his favorite Italian restaurant. They've agreed to let him take a cooking lesson, and it might be funny. And I think it might endear him to our target audience. If that's okay with you, and with Emma of course, I'll go tomorrow afternoon."

"Slow down." William drops the whiteboard eraser on its tray and rubs his hands together. "First, it's generally not appropriate to be on your phone during a meeting, but considering what's going on today, I get it. And second, that's not why I held you back."

"Okay." Sometimes I'm a dork. This is not new information, but it's a thing I need to remind myself once in a while, especially when I've been sufficiently dorky.

"I didn't see any of the footage with the kids from the children's hospital. Did you not get it edited?"

"Well . . . you see . . . here's the thing." I mentally cringe at how I sound. "I got one still shot of Gabe with the kids, but he asked me not to take any more pictures and not to post the one I did take. He felt like it was a little exploitative of the kids, which was why I struck the deal with him to do the piano footage and—"

"Coffee." William holds up a hand. "Next time give me a heads-up, okay? The piano footage is great, but it doesn't replace something that has community outreach appeal."

"Right. Yes. Sure. Sorry."

"Perfect. And, Coffee, one more thing."

"Two sugars and a dash of hazelnut?" I offer, hoping that it will relieve the tension a little.

A half smile tugs at his lips. "Is the joke getting old yet?"

On the inside, I'm groaning, but on the outside, I keep my face pleasant. "Not quite yet."

WHEN I WAS IN ELEMENTARY SCHOOL, MY CLASS DID A SCIENCE PROJ-ect where we raised caterpillars. We watched them hatch, fed them milkweed, and cheered when they started breaking out of their cocoons. On the day we released them, the interior of the butterflies' container trembled with activity. Dozens of new wings stretched and fluttered, occasionally taking flight and bumping into the net walls.

As I approach Moretti's, I'm fairly certain a butterfly science project is trapped inside my torso. My stomach practically shivers with excitement, and none of it has to do with Gabe.

Okay, fine. All of it has to do with Gabe, but only a little of it has to do with seeing him again. I really need this to go well so that it'll get me on William's good side.

I tamp down all flutters as I come in through the back entrance. Gabe is leaning against the counter, relaxed, nodding along to whatever Maria is saying in Italian. She's gesturing with her left hand, white towel tossed over her shoulder and a white apron tied around her waist. A man is doing dishes with a giant pull-down hose that looks like it belongs to a power washer, while another man in a black button-down coat and matching pageboy cap is chopping vegetables at light speed. I'd lose a finger doing that.

Gabe turns as I enter the kitchen, and I could totally be day-dreaming, but I swear he checks me out. I'm wearing the sleeveless black dress with the high collar and funky hemline from the day I crashed into him on the beach. I know it looks amazing on me, but I don't expect him to notice. Yet there's something about the way he looks at me that makes it hard to breathe.

Or maybe that's just the Gabriel Fortunato Effect.

Maria whips him with the towel. "Stop staring and go help her with those bags."

The man at the sink laughs without looking up from his duties, and Gabe snaps into action before Maria can smack him again. And while I'm strong enough to carry them, it is a relief to get the strap off my shoulder. Also, I wasn't imagining his gaze if Maria noticed it too.

"Thank you." I shake out my nearly numb fingers.

"Is that the dress you were wearing the day we met?" He sets the tripod on the table in the nook. There's a laugh in his voice when he says, "It looks different when you're on your feet."

"Haha. You're hysterical."

"I didn't mean that how it sounded. Well, I did a little." He holds his hands up like he's ready to ward off a blow, and Maria looks ready to deal out another towel whack on my behalf. "I meant it looks nice. You look nice in it. It looks nice on you."

I've never seen him flustered, and it's sort of adorable to see him off balance. And I wonder if it means anything or if I'm reading into it like a lit teacher and inferring something that isn't there.

"Shall we cook?" He fumbles with the zipper on the tripod bag. "Let's cook."

Maria insists I wear an apron and pull up my hair before I start filming, so Gabe puts together the tripod for me. Once everything is set, I drop my phone into the clamp and let Gabe work his magic.

He was right. Watching him cook is pretty funny. Maria is not a patient teacher, and their back and forth is hysterical, mostly in

English and occasionally in Italian when she gets frustrated with him. They make a traditional Neapolitan pizza, and she outlines the rules as they go. Rolling pins are not allowed, and watching Gabe attempt to hand toss the crust is maybe the best thing I've ever seen. For a minute, he forgets the camera is on, and his face crumples in concentration as he tries to match her technique. Once the dough is stretched to Maria's satisfaction, they don't simply slap marinara on it—or spaghetti sauce like we do at my house. Instead, they use homemade sauce from a special type of tomato. Fresh mozzarella and basil go on top of that.

"Olives." He snaps his fingers. "It needs olives."

Maria looks at him like he slapped her nonna. "Get out of my kitchen." She points toward the back door.

Gabe laughs, and when Maria realizes he's joking, she joins him. She puts one arm around his waist, and he kisses her on the side of the head just like he did with Iliana. It's so endearing that I can't help but grin. Which, if I'm being honest, is a little terrifying. Because this Gabe is really, really appealing.

Gabe's pizza is less round than the one Maria made, but the mozzarella is blistered on top and rises and falls in little valleys with bright chunks of crushed tomato breaking through. I wasn't hungry until Maria set it at the spot where I ate the last time I was here.

"Sit. Eat," she commands, and there's no way I'm turning her down.

"No, no, no." Gabe swaps Maria's pizza to his spot and hands me his lopsided one.

"Everyone's going to know that isn't the pizza you made. It's too even." I try to snatch the pizza back, but he grabs my wrist.

"That's not the point. I want to see your face when you eat *my* pizza."

I cock my head at him. "You're so sure it's going to be good?"

The arrogant grin is back. "Everything I do is good."

"*You're* awful."

"Tell me that after you've taken a bite." He pulls out his phone and focuses it on me. "I'm filming this for proof."

Maria teaches me that Neapolitan pizza is intended to be eaten like a libretto—a little book—folded in half. Which is super funny considering Chicago is famous for deep-dish pizza, and there's no way you can fold a slice of that.

"Here goes nothing," I say to Gabe's phone and take a bite. The flavor explodes across my tongue, and despite myself, I groan.

"Is it the best pizza you've ever had?" Gabe's eyes are sparkling with mischief as he sits across from me, leg pressed against mine. There's no simple brushing this time.

"I should say that it's awful, but—" I take another bite. "That would be a lie. It's delicious."

I grab my phone so I can film his response to Maria's pizza. He takes a bite, closing his eyes for a moment of delight. I know *that* expression isn't fake.

While he's mid-chew, I push my phone toward him, nibbling my bottom lip nervously. "Did you see this?"

He has the pizza halfway to his mouth, but he doesn't bite it again, considering the information on the screen.

"More than ten thousand likes in the first hour; more than eight hundred thousand in the first twenty-four." I can't stop myself from beaming. "ESPN retweeted it at noon. There's a huge chance it'll go viral."

He picks a piece of tomato off the edge of his pizza before it can fall and puts it on the platter. "Great."

Gabe is decidedly less enthusiastic than I'd hoped, and it's like a cold frost on my poor butterflies. "Are you worried about the comments? Because I've looked through them and everyone is so impressed." I scroll down, looking for a name with a checkmark beside it. "Look! That's the anchor from *Good Morning America*."

"I saw." He takes another bite, never once looking at me.

The butterflies are dead. Their poor little corpses are frozen pebbles at the bottom of my stomach. "You're not happy. You're mad."

He half tosses his pizza onto the plate. "I'm glad that people like watching me play the piano."

"There's a huge 'but' at the end of this sentence."

His mouth curls on one side. "I don't see any butts, especially huge ones."

He's trying to deflect with humor, but I'm not going to take the easy out he's offering. "But, you're embarrassed? You don't want everyone to know you play so well? You wished you'd kept your talent—"

"My mother saw it," he says bitterly.

Gabe has said very little about his family, but I remember our first conversation here. He didn't say anything specifically, but I got the sense that his relationship with his parents was difficult.

"Given the other things on Instagram, I don't think this is the worst thing she could have seen you doing."

That draws a real smile out of him, even if it is slightly unwilling. "That is probably true."

"So why are you all worked up?"

"You wouldn't understand."

"How do you know? I have parents that I struggle with from time to time." Which is sort of an understatement.

He looks up at me, conflict clear in his eyes. He lets out a long, slow breath before he speaks again. "My parents are—well, my mother mostly is—impossible to please. The first thing she said to me this morning was, 'How could you let yourself get so out of practice?'" He gives a cold-sounding laugh. "Ten thousand people commented that they were impressed, but my mother could only complain about my fingering in the twelfth measure. I explained that I've been a bit busy, trying to be a professional calcio player. And she said . . . 'Trying. Not succeeding.'"

I wince, feeling the pinch of her words. "Oh, Gabe. I'm so sorry. You know that's not true." I reach across the table and touch his forearm. "And honestly, who cares about what your mother says?"

"I do." His expression is so acidic it burns. "Although, at some point, I have to accept that I'll never do anything to please either of my parents."

"My problem with my mom is the complete opposite. She is so used to my brother Max succeeding that she seems almost surprised when *I* do. It's like she's waiting for me to fall or fail—sometimes both at once—" I make myself laugh to take the edge off my words. "So it seems like screwing up is inevitable."

He flips his hand over to cover mine, thumb tucked under my palm. "Why? You're so . . ." He pauses, and I worry what the next word might be. Spastic? Ridiculous? Accident-prone?

Instead he says, "Persistent. You don't give up easily."

"Ha. I'm choosing to take that as a compliment."

"As it was intended."

It seems my stomach butterflies have been revived by his kindness. "Are your parents as hard on Iliana as they are on you?"

"If anything, they're harder. She was an amazing dancer, but all their pushing finally backfired. She quit two years ago and hasn't stepped back into a studio." He runs a finger over my knuckles. "Without dance, she just seems so . . ."

"Lost?" I supply, when his silence stretches.

"Yes. Lost." A flush rises in his cheeks, and I don't think it has anything to do with the fire in the pizza oven. "Iliana never went to university; she doesn't have any skills. I invited her to come here and stay with me until she figured out what to do next, but . . ." He gives a different shrug this time, uncertain.

Usually, I have to pry information out of him, sorting through sarcasm and half-truths to figure out what's real, but maybe being in a kitchen with familiar food and people who care about him acts like a crowbar. "She's not really trying to figure anything out?" I ask.

His right leg starts bouncing, shaking the table a little. "Sometimes I want to kick her out—especially when she throws parties at my apartment—but she's my sister."

"And you love her even if she makes your life miserable sometimes?"

He nods slowly.

Despite Iliana's faults, she's a little piece of home to him. If I couldn't go home, if I couldn't speak to my parents, I'd totally cling to my brothers.

The image of Gabe walking out of the club, arm around Iliana's shoulders, pops into my head. "Wait a second. She was in Mexico with you. What happened that night?"

"It doesn't matter." He doesn't make eye contact.

"Were you defending her?" When he doesn't admit it, I pull my hand out from underneath his. "You *were*. Why didn't you say something? Telling the media the truth would totally change your part in that story." We wouldn't have to work quite as hard to change his image.

"Don't give me more credit than I deserve." His overconfident expression is back. "I promise I was not completely innocent in that fight."

"Still—"

"It's out of the news now. Let's leave it out, yeah?"

He's not wrong. It's better to move forward at this point. I agree half-heartedly.

"*But* if you want to make sure nothing like that happens at my charity banquet . . ." He pauses dramatically, barely keeping a grin from his lips. "Then you should be my date."

I roll my eyes. "Because you're planning to punch one of your teammates?"

He tilts his head to the side, considering. "I can't promise that I won't."

"You're making this more appealing by the second."

He puts his hand over his heart like he's making a solemn oath. "If you come as my date, I'll be on my very best behavior."

I let his story about Iliana slide through the sieve in my head, picking out the fragments that glimmer. Taking the media's heat to keep his sister out of the news is chivalrous, if stupid. And wanting to help her, albeit in the wrong way, is sweet. Underneath all that ego, it seems that Gabriel Fortunato is a pretty decent, if imperfect, guy.

When I don't answer right away, he leans both elbows on the table, donning an expression that is nothing short of a smolder. "The anticipation is killing me."

I weigh the consequences. He could do something stupid, but I doubt it because he's been working hard to correct his mistakes. It would be good for him to go with someone who's guaranteed not to cause a scene.

"Can I think about it?"

"Of course." The smile he gives me is the same one he gave Maria when they were cooking, wide and glimmering, making the room around us disappear. "You can give me your answer at my game on Thursday."

Seventeen

With most of Gabe's social media under control, I go back to regular intern duties: research, fetch someone coffee, make copies, get someone else coffee, go through tabloids with Katie, make more coffee. Mara seems to have forgotten that she hates me and is soaking up the praise for some clever copy she wrote for a press release. I go out to dinner with Katie on Wednesday night, take Watford for a long walk in the park, and go back to the Lily Pond to enjoy the peace and quiet there.

The piano video hit two million views just after lunch Thursday, and it looks like the cooking lesson with Maria will be a close second. I've got to figure out our next big thing.

I mean *Gabe's* next big thing. Not ours. There's no *our*. He only invited me to the game so I could get more footage. Probably. I think. He didn't exactly clarify in the dozens of slightly flirtatious work-related texts.

By the time I'm picking out my outfit for the game, I'm weirdly anxious to see him face-to-face. I guess it's because we're friends now. My friend is going to play soccer tonight. I want my friend to do well.

My friend is super hot and sometimes when we're together I forget my own name.

Scratch that. Gabe is a client and we have a good working relationship.

Good. Working. Relationship.

I ride the red line out to Soldier Field, then walk the last twenty minutes, planning to get my ticket and sit in a quiet corner, hopefully unnoticed, of the Media Deck. It's an open area with a great view of the field, and a perfect place to get some footage for Gabe's feeds. Lots of rich folks and big companies impress their guests with these seats, but it's also where all the coaches' and players' wives and girlfriends hang out. I wanted to wear a hat, but Emma gave that a hard no. She wanted me to wear a Fortunato jersey, but I don't want to draw any attention to myself. Instead, I chose a simple white peasant top with ruffled sleeves and the one pair of jeans I own that fit me perfectly. I think it's a pretty casual combination, but not too casual.

Once I enter the suite, I realize I've hit the perfect note. There are middle-aged white dudes in khaki cargos and polo shirts, a handful of professional-looking younger people in office attire, and some beautiful women either in sundresses or jerseys and jeans. Em said that WAGs—wives and girlfriends of the players—would cover the fashion spectrum throughout the season.

Not that I fall into that category by any means.

I take a seat in a leather chair in the far corner and drop my purse in the chair next to me, hoping people will think it's occupied. There's a big flat-screen hanging just a few feet from me, so I see the game better than I can over the railing. My purse trick works because I'm left in my corner all by myself.

Just like every other soccer game I've ever watched, both the home and opposing teams walk onto the field holding the hands of little kids from local soccer programs. Gabe is paired with a girl with the cutest pom-pom pigtails. She looks up at him with undisguised devotion. He boops her on the nose, and she laughs and hugs his leg.

I remember worshipping a soccer player like that once. Back when The Cheating Bastard was still Uncle Geoff and played for the English National team, they held a friendly match here in Chicago. He must have pulled all the strings because we had seats almost on the field. We met Geoff after, and he gave me a game jersey that smelled like grass and sweat, but I wore it anyway because I was eight or nine and he was my hero. He and Emma had rented a big cabin in Michigan, and we spent the rest of the week there, riding Jet Skis, fishing, and having the best vacation of my life.

It makes me feel horrible, but sometimes I think it would have been easier if he'd left Aunt Emma a widow. It's not that Uncle Geoff should be dead by any means—he doesn't deserve that—but then I could mourn the man I imagined him being instead of missing the man I thought he was.

The first half of the game is ugly. Seb blocks seven shots on goal, but two sneak past him, and our offense can't get anything going. Our players make stupid passes and don't clear the ball from the box. Gabe gets slide tackled and jumps to his feet, clearly pissed that it didn't draw a card.

"That's a yellow," I say half to myself and half to the ref who can't possibly hear me. "Come on! Book him!" I'm not the only person yelling at the field, so I don't feel ridiculous that I've gotten sucked into the game.

By halftime, the Media Deck is filling up. People are leaning against the railing and sitting in every chair, except the one next to me. A woman I know I've seen somewhere sits next to my purse. She gives me a little wave, and I smile back.

The team returns after halftime with a new attack and looking fresh. Gabe is keyed in. His footwork is so fast that no one can keep up with him. He intercepts passes meant for the opposition, and he always seems to be in the right place at the right time. But despite everything, he can't get a clean shot.

My teeth hurt from clenching my jaw in anxiety. Just before my molars are ground to nubs, he manages to punch one over the goalie's head. I jump to my feet, cheering out loud.

The woman beside me is on her feet too and gives me a double high five. "Are you here for Gabe?"

"Oh no! I mean, yes, but not like in a romantic sense or anything. I work on his social media stuff. Actually, I'm an intern for his publicist. So I just follow directions."

Nicely handled. The lady doth protest too much, methinks. Why can't I use Gabe's favorite communication method and shrug my way through life?

She laughs. "I'm Blanca. Seb's girlfriend." She waves toward the goal. "You're Maddie?"

Oh my gosh, why does Seb's girlfriend know my name?

"Don't look so shocked. We had Gabe over for dinner last week and he said nice things about you. He mentioned you'd be here today. I'm glad someone is here to see him play. He's had a rough go of it after the World Cup and all."

"Yeah, I bet." My happiness that Gabe talked about me fades. He's a world-class talent, and his family never watches him play. Not even his sister, who lives here.

It's the eighty-eighth minute, and we're still down by one, when Gabe gets a long pass that's just barely onside. Watching him dribble down the field—even though I know it's only a matter of seconds—stretches into a painful eternity before he shoots left-footed. It skids under the goalie's glove.

I'm on my feet, Blanca's holding my wrist, and we're screaming together. "Two goals!" Fans bang their drums, yelling his name, as he slides on his knees into the corner. His teammates practically attack him, piling on to celebrate. As he gets to his feet, he faces the suite, kisses two fingers, and—it could be my imagination—points them right at me.

It's ridiculous, but the little motion hits me like an arrow through the chest. I press my free hand to the spot just above my heart.

"You're sure you're not here in a romantic sense?" Blanca gives me a huge grin.

"I think it was to the crowd."

"If you say so."

I excuse myself to get a drink because I'd gotten so sucked into the game that I forgot to eat. Most everything has been cleaned up, but I manage to grab a water bottle. As I turn, I feel someone staring at me.

His forehead is wrinkled in confusion, like he's trying to solve a math problem. I guess $a^2 + b^2 = c^2$ because I see the solution pop into his eyes.

"Maddie?" he says, grin spreading across his face. "Is that you?"

I swallow the grit that's suddenly filled my throat. "Hey, Uncle Geoff."

Eighteen

I ALWAYS IMAGINED THAT WHEN I SAW THE CHEATING BASTARD again that I'd tell him exactly what I thought about him. Most of those words were things I'd never be allowed to say in public. Or anywhere, really.

Instead of angry, I'm tired. And, honestly, a little sad. He looks exactly the same, low to the ground and sturdy, all wide shoulders and square face.

"Em told me I may run into you here."

I wish she would have mentioned it to me, then I wouldn't have come.

Oh. That's probably why she didn't tell me. Curse you, Emma. "Yeah, I'm here for—" I motion toward the field like that's an explanation. Please let him think that means the game.

Geoff steps closer, shaking his head in astonishment. "You got so tall. You're a proper giant now."

It was a joke we all shared. He was our "gnome" and we were his "proper giants." It's not as funny now as it was when I was ten, but it does bring back good memories.

"Em didn't mention you'd be here tonight."

"To catch a game and watch a player. Some things never change."

And some things can never be the same. My eyes flick to the pitch, looking for something emotionally safe to land on. The players are mingling, and I realize I missed the last two minutes of the game. I guess it ended in a tie. "I . . . I should go down." I hook my thumb over my shoulder to indicate the field.

He nods, lips pressing thin. "It was good to see you."

"You too." And I realize that I mean it. We exchange an awkward sort of hug, and I feel his loss even more potently. Uncle Geoff used to give rib-crushing hugs that would pick your feet up off the floor, but The Cheating Bastard gives soft shoulder pats.

As he steps back, he says, "I wish things would have gone differently."

They could have. "That makes two of us."

"Give your family my love."

No way. "Enjoy Chicago while you're here." Then he heads back to the table he was sitting at—with Scott, who raises his glass at me in hello.

Geoff is with Scott.

A bell chimes in my head. I grab my purse from its spot next to Blanca and google Geoff's name. *Retired Premier League player Geoffrey Jones is expected to be tapped to manage his former team when the current manager retires at the end of the season.*

He's here for Gabe. He has to be. Who else on the team could he be scouting? Who else on this team does Scott represent?

Oh my gosh. This is Gabe's chance to get back to Europe.

"You better go down and say hello." Blanca grabs my arm and leads me to the door. "I'm positive Gabe knows you're here, but he'll want to see you anyway."

I don't argue, letting her tow me down the stadium stairs. I'm so shocked about seeing Geoff and Scott together that I don't even worry about tripping and rolling all the way to the safety bars that stop drunks from falling onto the field.

Gabe is signing jerseys and autographs near the tunnel that leads to the team's locker room. I'm not sure how he picks me out of the crowd, but he hands an autograph back to a kid and jogs over to me.

"You're still here!" He hauls himself up, wedging his cleats beneath the bottom rail. He reaches for me and I go easily into his embrace because I'm afraid he's going to slip backward and crack his head open on the cement and die. Also, because it's really hard not to hug a gorgeous—if slightly sweaty—guy who's glad to see you.

"Your second shot was pretty lucky," I say into his shoulder, keeping a tight fistful of his shirt, one more safeguard to save him from an untimely death.

"That was pure skill." His leans back but leaves his arms around my waist. Happiness sparkles from his eyes. I don't know if it's the result of a two-goal game or because I'm here. And I can't decide which one I want it to be.

"The announcers said that you've got a boot like no other, but they're biased." I roll my eyes like it was no big deal.

"What about that beautiful cross?"

"Do you need me to tell you you're amazing?" I nod toward the impatient fans. "I'm pretty sure you have plenty of people who will do that for you."

"Which is why I need you." He brushes his lips across my cheek, chaste and unassuming. "Someone has to keep me humble."

It was nothing. Less than nothing. He's Italian. They kiss everyone, but my whole body twinges with his touch.

Gabe drops to the ground, completely unaware of his effect on me. "Meet me downstairs after? I'm starving. Let's get dinner."

He jogs backward, fake impatience on his face as he waits for my answer.

"If I have to."

The smile he gives me in response makes my stomach turn to jelly.

I LOITER AGAINST THE WALL OUTSIDE THE LOCKER ROOM, LETTING the media get their sound bites and footage before sliding in after all the friends and family.

And Gabe's agent.

Scott is leaning toward Gabe, voice low—conscious of the still-lingering reporters—but his hand is chopping to punctuate a sentence I can't hear.

I imagined Gabe would be practically bursting out of his skin. He could be playing for Arsenal after the trade window opens. But he's got his foot propped up on the bench, adjusting a bag of ice plastic-wrapped around his ankle. There's no fake smile. No media-ready Gabriel Fortunato. He straightens, posture perfect, spine rigid. He looks more like he's ready for a fight.

This is not good.

I know it's not quite La Liga—but the salaries are always good and it's more competitive than here. Why is he not happy?

Edging a little closer, I hear Scott say, "You have got to be realistic about this."

And even though I don't know the agent that well, I swear there's an undercurrent in his body language, a tenseness in his massive shoulders.

"I am being realistic." Gabe's tone is flat, focusing on his ankle. "My answer is no."

"At least listen to him," Scott continues, telegraphing "be nice" with his eyes. "I suggested Moretti's for dinner tonight. You game?"

You know those cartoon characters whose faces get redder and redder until fire bursts from their ears? Gabe is the human equivalent of that. "I can't believe you'd even consider it."

"Now, you hold your horses—"

"Hi!" I say, way too loudly. Both of their heads whip toward me. "Scott! It's so good to see you. Again. Wasn't that a great game? It was such a good game. Gabe you played so well. You hit the ball perfectly."

Nice, Mads.

I sound like an idiot, but my blabbering throws them off for a second. Long enough for me to face Gabe. "Are we still on to film those clips tonight? I know you're getting ready for your road trip, and I'd love to have them before you leave so we can keep the ball rolling, social media–wise." I turn to face Scott. "I don't know if you heard, but Gabe's Instagram videos have gotten an immense response."

Gabe's confusion is enough to diffuse the bomb that was about to explode in his head. "Clips." It sounds like a question to my ears. "Yes. Right. We had plans to film clips." He nods at his agent. "I'm sorry. I have other plans."

Now Scott's the one with the short fuse. "Gabe, Geoff has come all the way from the UK to talk to you. Maddie will have to get some 'clips' later."

That's funny, I thought Geoff came to see Watford. I don't say that out loud. I took my shot, and now the ball is figuratively at Gabe's feet.

"Tell Mr. Jones I'm not interested in anything he has to say."
Gabe holds his hand out to me.

Okay, so that's how we're playing this. I step to Gabe's side, slipping my fingers between his. His grip is so tight that I can feel his pulse racing, hard and fast. "Let's go, Madeline."

The blood vessel on Scott's right temple is about to rupture. There's no other way to explain why it's throbbing that hard. "This conversation is not over."

"As my agent, you should have known it was a conversation we would never have." Gabe throws his bag over his shoulder and half drags me out of the room. I look back right as we push through the door, and Scott's staring after us, face beet red. Not good.

"What just happened?" I ask, once we're out to the parking area. No one's close enough to make me worry about being overheard.

"I just told the future manager of Arsenal and the biggest agent in sports to *vai a quel paese*," Gabe says as he opens the passenger side door for me.

"I have no idea what that means, but yes." My stomach is bubbling nervously, but I also think I might burst out laughing. "Should I have stayed out of it? You looked like you were going to punch Scott, and he looked like he might strangle you, and there were still reporters and I was worried that they'd catch it on camera, and it would be all over the news. But then when I started talking, Scott looked like he wanted to kill me. I mean, he's got fists the size of oven mitts, so he could probably take both of us out at the same time."

I cover my mouth with both hands and lean back against the side of the Ferrari. "Did I do the wrong thing?"

Gabe pulls my hands down, holding on to my wrists. "Scott tried to ambush me, and you saved me with your . . . talking."

"Why would Scott ambush you?"

He grimaces. "Food first, then explanation."

G ABE AND I SNEAK THROUGH THE DIM LOBBY OF THE B ELDEN-Stratford and into the gold elevator with two bags of greasy take-out. The front desk receptionist doesn't say anything, more interested in the romance novel she's got on her desk than us.

He didn't want to go back to his apartment, afraid Iliana might have brought home guests. I certainly couldn't take him back to Emma's place. She might balk at me bringing a client home. Even if it is just to eat Chinese food.

Instead of stopping at the top floor of apartments, we ride the elevator all the way to the sundeck. It usually closes at eleven, but when Emma gave me the key to her apartment, she also gave me one to the sundeck. It's one of the perks of owning space in the building, instead of just renting it.

Gabe drags a small side table between two lounge chairs, and we sit across from each other and open our boxes.

"That smells delicious. What did you get?" He leans forward to see into my box, but besides the lights from the facade of the building and the streetlights far below, it's almost impossible to see.

"Vegetable lo mein."

"No meat?" He grimaces.

"You ordered enough for five people." I reach toward his box with my chopsticks, and he slaps them down. "I'm offended. I can't have one bite?"

"Italians do not share."

I'm shocked. "You're making that up. Didn't Italians invent family-style eating?"

Even in the dim light, I can see the disgust on his face. "Family-style means our meals are served from the same container. We do *not* eat off the same plate."

"You're not eating off a plate." I snatch a piece of orange beef and pop it in my mouth. "I scooped it out of your container."

He leans halfway across the table. "You'll pay for that."

I give him my most innocent smile. "I am not afraid of you."

Gabe coughs into his elbow, choke-laughing. "Most people would be."

"I'm not most people."

"I've noticed."

I look at him, and he looks back. The imaginary thread connecting us ratchets tighter. These moments have got to stop.

I clear my throat and tip my box to scoop some noodles directly into my mouth because I'm sexy like that. "So you were going to tell me about Scott's ambush?"

He returns total focus to his dumplings. "No business while eating."

"Please." I poke his arm with a chopstick. "I thought we were friends."

"We are." He says it fast, like he doesn't even question it anymore. It feels nice that we've crossed that threshold. "Geoff Jones wants to negotiate a deal that could result in me playing for Arsenal."

"And that's *bad*?"

He shrugs, switching to my noodles. I don't make any comment about his refusal to share earlier. Hypocrite.

"Do you know you do that a lot?"

"Do what?"

I mimic his shrug. "That's not an answer. That's a subject change or redirection, but I jumped into a conversation I wasn't really a part of tonight because we are *friends* and I deserve an explanation for why you needed to be rescued."

"Is there any grammar in your spoken sentences?"

"Stop. Changing. The subject." I throw a couple noodles at him in frustration, and he picks one off his shirt and flicks it back at me, grinning in a way that makes something in my chest swirl.

Ugh. He's done it again. "You were telling me about Geoff and Arsenal."

Gabe sighs and sets down his chopsticks. "Geoff and I have history, and I'd rather play anywhere than for him."

"He retired before you started playing professionally. How could you possibly have history?"

"He was one of the announcers for the World Cup Final. After I missed the goal . . . he said I choked in a high-stakes moment. That I was another Adu, a Macheda, a player who entered the league too young and would never live up to the hype." Gabe rests his elbows on his knees and keeps his focus between his feet. "*Everyone* believed him. The media. The fans. Even my parents. And then when I was in the car accident, Geoff said it was proof that he was right about me. That I was too young, too immature. That I was imploding under the pressure."

I cringe. The Geoff I knew was never that cold, that callous, but it sounds exactly like something The Cheating Bastard would say.

"I'm sorry." I turn my knees toward him and take both of his hands. "But if Geoff wants you to play for him, couldn't that be a good thing? Like showing the world that what he said was wrong?"

"When I lay out all the details, I know, logically, this is a step closer to where I want to be. And yet, the thought of playing for him . . ."

He doesn't finish the sentence. He doesn't have to. How hard would it be to be coached by the person whose commentary led to your nightmares? To face that person every single day? To wonder if he'd throw you under the bus if you had a bad game? I understand how hard it would be to say all of that aloud, so this time I change the subject. "Did they give us fortune cookies?"

Gabe fishes in the bottom of a brown paper sack and comes up with six plastic-wrapped cookies and a dozen packets of soy sauce.

"*Ooo!*" I take one of the sugary treats. "They were generous today."

"You did say I ordered enough to feed five people."

"True."

I crack mine open, breaking a piece to put in my mouth and pulling out the little message. It's too dark, so I shine my phone's flashlight on it and immediately shake my head.

"What does it say?" he asks, dropping all the garbage into the bag.

"'Work on improving your exercise routine.'"

"Don't listen to that cookie. You're perfect." He snatches the paper out of my hand and drops it in with the leftovers. "Try this one."

I open the next one, pretending he didn't call me perfect in a totally offhand way. "These fortune cookies suck. 'Be kind to pigeons.' What kind of fortune is that?" I shake my head. "What does yours say?"

"My phone's dead." He moves around the table and drops next to me so he can use mine. He crumples his cookie in his palm and fishes the paper out of the bits. "Go—"

He stiffens and folds the fortune in half and shoves it in his pocket. "You're right. These fortune cookies are stupid." He shakes the crumbs into his mouth.

"Rude!" I bump him with my elbow. "I read both of mine to you."

"I'll pick another one."

"No! I want to know what that one said." I reach toward his pocket, but he tips sideways, hiding it between his body and the chair.

"You big baby." I throw another fortune cookie at him, and he catches it before it hits the deck. "You have to read it out loud this time. It's a rule."

"Are you the boss of fortune cookies now?"

"I always have been." I lean close so that I can see the paper as soon as it's out of the wrapper. My shoulder is wedged against his side, and I'm holding the phone so he'll have to put the fortune where we can both see it.

He pulls the slip out of the cookie without breaking it and reads, "Go for it."

Everything goes perfectly still for a moment, like a movie I've paused. I can see us on the screen in my head, sitting on a Chicago rooftop late at night, sharing the same reclining chair. I've gotten so comfortable with the hugs, the cheek kiss, the closeness between us, that I hadn't even registered that the heat of his body is keeping me from shivering every time the breeze rises off the lake.

"Hmmm." I flick off the flashlight, plunging the roof into sudden darkness, but I know his eyes are on me. "What do you think that is supposed to mean?"

"It was the same fortune both times." He turns sideways to face me completely, hand falling on top of mine, knuckles dragging slowly up my forearm, fingers opening against the back of my neck. "Seems more significant twice in a row, no?"

He's asking about more than fortune cookies; he's asking for a sign. If I want to pull away, he's giving me every opportunity.

I don't. I want to stay right here, in this moment, where it's just us and the moonlight. I want his hands on me and his lips on mine. I want to be closer.

"It definitely seems . . . " I say, leaning in infinitesimally. It doesn't take much to line my mouth up with his. "Significant."

The first kiss is a simple brush of his lips against mine. I pull back a little, heart thundering in the base of my throat. He doesn't let me go far, shifting his hand so that it cradles my face before he kisses me again. The second kiss is nothing like the first. It's everything that I associate with Gabriel Fortunato—heat, hunger, and self-confidence.

His lips part against mine, kissing me like this is his native language. My arms wrap tight around him, hands skimming up his back, while his slide down mine. Those musician's fingers press against the knobs of my spine, the gaps between my ribs, sending shivery arpeggios all the way to my toes.

Five minutes pass, ten, a million, and we're lying side by side on the chair, legs intertwined. His lips have discovered the underside of my jaw, then the dip of my collarbone, when my phone rings. And it jolts me back to reality.

What am I doing? What am I *doing*?

I'm making out with Gabriel Fortunato on the roof of my aunt's apartment building.

I try to ignore both the phone and my rising sense of panic, but Gabe gives me a quick kiss just under my ear and asks, "You going to answer that?"

It's a good enough excuse to buy myself some headspace. "I probably should."

The call drops to voice mail, but a text pops through almost immediately.

Emma: I forgot to give you a curfew. But I'm giving you one, and it's right now.

"I don't think I've ever had a curfew." Gabe's propped up on his elbow, looking down at me. "It must be nice to have someone worrying about whether or not you'll come home."

That's one way to look at it. "I guess I better go."

He pulls me back for one more kiss that stretches far longer than I intend it to. Kissing him is something I definitely should not be doing and something I definitely don't want to stop.

"By the way," he says against my lips. "Have you thought about coming with me to the gala?"

"So that's what this is all about. You're trying to convince me to be your date." His teeth graze my bottom lip and I forget what I was saying.

Until my phone buzzes again.

Emma: I know where you are. Don't make me come get you.

That does the job.

Me: On my way.

I walk Gabe down to the lobby, giving him one last goodbye kiss before riding the elevators up to Emma's apartment by myself. I smooth my hair as best I can, but there's nothing I can do for the bee-stung lips and dazed look in my eyes.

I expect the apartment to be dark when I swing open the door, but every light is on. And while Emma's dressed for bed, she's not alone. She's on one end of the lavender couch, Watford curled around her feet. And Scott is overfilling one of the white wingback chairs.

"Whoa." I stop in the entryway. "What is he doing here?"

He looks at Emma, and she flicks her hand at me, telling him to go ahead.

Scott stands. "Maddie, we need to talk."

CHAPTER

Nineteen

"I'M NOT ASKING FOR MUCH," Scott says, ignoring the fact that I'm not even looking at him.

I'm scratching behind Watford's ears. He abandoned Emma to come lean against my legs, and I'm grateful for the distraction. Everything about this situation makes me feel gross. Scott called Emma after our run-in at the stadium, and absolutely had to talk to us *tonight*. She set up this trap—there's really no other way to describe it—although she called it an intervention.

"You have more sway with Gabe than anyone else." Scott leans forward in the chair, and the fur on Watford's back bristles. "He does more for you than he has for any publicist in his entire career. Just ask him to meet with Geoff. You know it's in his best interest."

All of Scott's arguments make it sound like playing for Arsenal really is the best step for Gabe's future. Money aside, the level of competition and the opportunities for sponsorships are so much better. If he stays in Chicago, there's a good chance he'll never reach his potential. Which would also prove that Geoff was right.

I smooth down Watford's coat, but it does nothing for my own emotions.

"He's in a pattern of self-sabotage. Help him get out of it."

"I don't know why you think I can convince him. Gabe makes up his own mind."

Scott looks at Emma for help, and she rubs her eyes tiredly. "I spent the last *year* trying to convince Gabe that we could change his public image, but he balked at everything. He pushed back on every idea or got himself in more trouble." She stands up and crosses the room, arms folded tight. "This time, he might have been really worried the Fire would get rid of him, but after that day at Velocity—when I saw the way he looked at you—I knew he'd agree because it was a chance to work with *you*. He likes you, Mads, and it shows."

He likes you and it shows. Those words should make me bubble, but instead I'm weighed down with guilt. Em never tried to hide the fact that my age made me an asset on his account, but I thought at some level she trusted me to work with Gabe because I was good at something. But really, she'd just found the right carrot.

"I know how much he hates Geoff. We talked about it tonight." My voice sounds threaded too tight, too high. "So, you're asking me to do something that seems a little underhanded."

"Your mom used to yell at you to ice your ankles after—"

"I don't see how that's got anything to do with this, Em." *And it's incredibly embarrassing that you brought it up in front of Scott.* I shoot a sideways look at the agent, but she ignores it.

"But it is. Sometimes we don't want to do what's best for us because it's uncomfortable." She puts her hand on the arm of my chair, reaching for my hand but falling short. "Geoff is willing to apologize personally, but he can't do it if Gabe refuses to meet with him."

Their eyes are heavy on me, waiting for a response.

"Having Gabe on a larger, more powerful team would also be good for Velocity." Emma changes tactics. "Which would ultimately be good for you."

Right. That's why I started this whole thing in the first place. She's certainly good at figuring out where everyone's buttons are. Going to UNC is mine, and apparently, for some unknown reason, I'm Gabe's.

"I don't want to pull you off this account—especially when you've been doing so well—simply because you've forgotten our goal and yours."

Geez, Em. Way to lay down the threat. Mom would be proud.

"I haven't forgotten." My voice snaps in a way that would have gotten me in trouble at home. If Emma hears it, she doesn't make a comment about my attitude. "But I can't promise that anything I say will make a difference."

"But you'll try?" Em asks.

"If I have to."

Emma and Scott exchange a relieved look, and I want to throw up.

"Thank you, Maddie."

"Whatever. I'm going to bed. Good night." I hurry to my room before they can call me back and flop face-first onto my bed.

I didn't trip over anything or fall down a flight of stairs, but it hasn't stopped me from stumbling. Am I putting aside my goals for a guy? For a throwaway summer fling?

Gabriel Fortunato is an international heartbreaker. I know that. The whole world knows that. It was one kiss on the rooftop. It didn't mean anything.

Yes, it did, my mind so kindly supplies. My heart kicks into sixth gear as I think about our conversations, about those moments of connection that have nothing to do with how good he looks. I don't think anyone knows how difficult his relationship with his family is, or that he manufactures charm for the public, or that if he was left to his own devices, he'd play the piano and nerd out over history.

Seeing the other side of him, the one that he doesn't put on for the cameras, is like being let in on a secret. It's a trust I want to keep.

A paw scratches my bedroom door.

"Ugh. Go away, Watford."

He scratches twice more and then whines. It's so pitiful, I can't ignore it. I swing open the door, and let him in. He hops onto the bed beside me, resting his head on my stomach.

Gosh, I love this stupid dog.

I MUST HAVE SHUT MY ALARM OFF BECAUSE I DON'T WAKE UP UNTIL I hear Watford gagging in the living room. And waking up late to a puking dog should have given me a trajectory of my day.

Patty snorts at me as I walk through the secret door, but it's such a typical Patty greeting that warning bells don't start chiming until Katie sees me. I swear it's like someone unplugged one of those Christmas yard inflatables—everything bright and sparkly about her goes dark, and she starts to sag.

"What's wrong?" I ask, feet skidding to a stop.

"It's not a big deal." She forces her smile into place, but it has none of its glitter. She loops her arm through mine and walks me to my cubicle. "Seriously, don't let it get to you."

I gasp. Every flat surface is decorated with color printouts—all pictures of me and Gabe from last night.

There's one from the parking lot, when I leaned against the Ferrari and Gabe had grabbed my wrists. It looks intense and kind of sexy, even though that's not at all how that moment felt.

There's another taken from the entrance of the Belden-Stratford.

Were there even guests in the lobby last night? I obviously didn't notice because in the picture, I'm one hundred percent focused on Gabe. We're hand in hand; I'm giving him an openmouthed grin.

The worst picture of all—or the best, if you're judging by artistic merit and not level of embarrassment—is taped right above my computer. Gabe and I are pressed together, only the safety bar at the field keeping us apart. He's smiling down at me. My hand is twisted in his shirt, baring a couple inches of his skin. From the way it's cropped, you can't tell that I'm holding onto him for balance and not because I want to peel his clothes off.

"That one's everywhere." Mara stands in my cubicle door, hands stuffed in her pockets of a sleeveless emerald jumpsuit. "Almost all the fan sites and the online gossips have it. It's steamy."

I bunch it in my hand, crumpling it into a tight ball that matches the one inside my chest. "Did you do this?"

She shrugs. "I came in early and decided to run all the searches. This is just part of what I found."

"So you hung them up all over my cubicle?"

"Oh, come on, Maddie. I'm just trying to help you out." Her smile is knife-edged as she hands me a file. "Don't you want to know *exactly* what people are saying about you and Fortunato?"

I open the cover, and it's full of page after page of comments printed from fan sites and gossip blogs. Very few of them are flattering. A lot of them are offensive.

"Is she one of those models who look absolutely rubbish unless they're made up?"

"She's not even that cute, so she must have money."

"What could he possibly see in her?"

Katie snatches them out of my hands, folds the stack in half, and hurls it Frisbee-style into Mara's cubicle. "Not helpful, Mara."

"Of course it is. Half our job is to be aware of what people are saying about our clients. I'm helping you become aware so you can deal with it appropriately before it turns into something else." She motions to the ball of paper in my fist. "And if *this* is the way you're going to go about handling the Fortunato account, at least own up to your methods."

When she drops into her chair, Katie makes finger guns at Mara's back.

"Ignore her," Katie says, scrolling through the feed for the @proWAGs account on Instagram. "Mara's just jealous and so are all of these idiots."

Commenters hack on each woman's hairstyle, body type, and outfit and slight them for things not even in the picture. The majority of the comments are women cutting down other women.

"Why do we do this to each other?" I ask, looking up from Katie's phone.

"You'd think we'd be beyond this sort of ugliness. Some women do such a good job building each other up, while others only see one seat at the table, and they want it for themselves." She shakes her head and leans against my desk. "We'd be so much better off if we worked toward the same goal instead of in competition with each other."

"Hear! Hear!" Arman says just loud enough for us to hear over the half wall that separates his desk from mine.

Katie climbs onto my desk so she can peer into Arman's space. "Have you been listening to everything we say?"

I can't see him, but I hear his laugh. It's pleasant and friendly, just like Arman.

"It's not like you ladies are whispering." He stands up so I can see his face. "For what it's worth . . ." He pauses to shoot a look toward

Mara's cubicle and lowers his voice even further. "I think, in her own way, she really is trying to help you."

At that moment, my desk phone rings. My aunt wants to see me in her office. Right away.

THERE'S AN OPEN FILE ON HER DESK. PICTURES OF ME AND GABE ARE shuffled in with news reports and screenshots from some gossipy fan sites. I didn't tell Emma about the rooftop episode, but from the photos I'm pretty sure she's made an educated guess.

"You wanted to see me?" I drop into one of the chairs in front of her desk and tuck my hands under my thighs.

"Did you approve the post Gabe uploaded this morning?" She holds up her phone so I can see the screen.

Two matching fortunes are placed on what appears to be his kitchen counter. I pretend not to see the line of out-of-focus bottles just off to the left—one bearing the unmistakable shape of Patrón tequila—and some lime wedges. Em makes no comment on the alcohol, which I guess is a bonus because I don't want to have to try to explain that.

Instead, I lean in close to see the picture. *Go for it*, both fortunes read. And the text below it says, "Some things are too good to pass up."

It could mean anything. It's ambiguous and unspecific, but that doesn't stop me from flashing hot with the memory of last night.

Em's eyebrows are up, waiting for an answer.

"No, I didn't approve this. And he *knows* he's supposed to run everything past me before he posts."

"I'm not upset about the post. It's a little enigmatic, which some fans really love. I'm more interested in what it's referring to. Do you have any idea?"

I have a pretty good guess, but I'm not admitting that now. Or possibly ever. "I'm not positive." Not completely a lie. I don't have any idea what he was thinking the *moment* he posted this picture.

"Hmm. I was reading too much into it, then. I was hoping that it meant he was willing to consider a move to Arsenal."

Or maybe it was the push he needed to kiss me until my head spun.

I open my mouth and then rethink what I was about to say. "You know Gabe blames Geoff for all the hate he got in Europe? That he choked during the World Cup?"

"I believe Geoff's quote was 'Fortunato is a young star who will flame out before we ever see his brilliance. Don't waste your money hoping he'll shine.' He repeated a similar phrase in every World Cup interview. He probably thought he sounded *so* clever." She smirks and shakes her head. "I understand Gabe's hard feelings, but Geoff is willing to figuratively eat crow on this. Gabe's biggest detractor wants to sign him for the team he's building. Is there *any* better way to reverse the damage of Geoff's remarks?"

I can't help but agree. I don't think Gabe would get a much bigger apology.

"Tell him that. Use the influence you have over him to get him to see sense." She taps the stack of pictures of me and Gabe. "You clearly have some."

Her words hollow out my chest. "I'm sort of wondering about the ethics and professionalism of this because Mara . . ."

"What did Mara say?"

I shake my head, feeling like Cube tattling on Max for eating the last ice cream sandwich. "She . . . umm . . . pointed out that mixing business with pleasure doesn't look very professional. And it's all business, I swear." Don't oversell it. I mentally slap myself.

Emma breaks into a huge smile. "Do you remember who I dated before Geoff?"

Hazily, I remember someone before The Cheating Bastard. "A baseball player? A pitcher for the Yankees?"

"I met him while I was working at that PR firm in New York. He had social anxiety disorder and needed someone to accompany him to events. Someone who could guide conversations to topics he felt comfortable with and could cover for him if he started to panic."

"I didn't know any of that."

"That's the point. He needed me as a buffer, and really, we're using you to the same end. Gabe just needs a little help getting out of his own way. If people want to assume there's something else, then let them assume."

A buffer. Okay. I can handle that. In fact, it almost sounds noble. Like I'm helping him overcome something that's stopping him from reaching his potential.

"He asked me to be his date to the gala. Do you think—"

"I think that's perfect. You were going to be there anyway, and now you'll have an excuse to stick by him all night and make sure he stays out of trouble." She looks me up and down, taking in my pink sundress and ponytail. "Plus having him show up with someone who isn't an heiress or a model will be really appealing to the public. They'll love seeing him with someone normal."

I ignore the way the last words sting. "Then, I guess, I'll tell him yes."

"All the interns will be involved in the set-up process, so it might be best if you meet Gabe there. William will be out front to lead Gabe through the media gamut. I don't see any issues with you joining him there."

Media. Gamut. Are there two less attractive words?

"Or I could just wait inside," I say hopefully.

"You could, but I don't think Gabe would have asked you to be his date if he wanted to show up alone."

"Right. Sure." I stand up from the chair and brush imaginary crumbs off my dress. "Was that all you needed?"

"Sweetie, I can tell you're still a little worried. Some people hold on to the antiquated idea that personal and professional lives should never overlap, but it's completely ridiculous. When you work as closely as we do with our clients, there's bound to be some cross-over." She holds her arms out, signaling to her fancy office. "It *is* how I got here."

She's built an amazing career out of the ashes of her marriage. But is this really something we should thank Geoff for?

Twenty

I HAVE A HARD TIME FOCUSING WHEN I GET BACK TO MY DESK. My stomach is tied in knots when I think about talking to Gabe about Geoff. Is going back to Europe really in his best interest? I mean, it obviously is money-wise. But if the public shamers bother Gabe so badly, then wouldn't it be better for him to stay here where he's relatively anonymous?

Since it's a half day, Katie and I skip our lunch break and decide to eat at Water Tower Place after work. The food hall has the world's best macaroni and cheese, which I get with a huge slice of fresh corn bread. Katie gets a kale salad, and we take our meals out to sit in the shadow of the Hancock Building.

"Heeey." Katie drops onto the bench next to me. She's wearing a floral-printed dress that looks straight out of the '90s. It even has lace around the collar. "You've been weirdly quiet today."

"I'm always quieter than you."

She scoffs. "True, but . . ." She digs her phone out of a striped bag that is big enough to double as a circus tent. "Is it this?"

It's the WAGs Instagram feed, and the top post is me and Blanca, cheering Gabe's second goal. We're both ecstatic. Neither of us knew cameras were on us. My eyes immediately drop to the first comment.

Somebody teach that girl to contour.

I put the phone screen down on the bench. "Do you follow this account—"

"Ugh," she interrupts. "No. Mara sent it to me."

"Why?"

She sighs and tucks her legs underneath. I've finally realized that this quirk is because she's so short her feet don't always touch the floor.

"She's totally got it out for you."

"I noticed." I'm hesitant to say anything about Mara out loud, but I really want Katie's take. "Do you think Mara would have deleted my video footage?"

"I think . . ." She pauses, pulling her enormous cat-eye sunglasses down over her eyes. "Maybe? It is a pretty awful thing to do, but she is banking on getting hired permanently after she graduates college. She feels like everyone has gotten help from their family, and she's got no one on her side."

"And by everyone she means me, right?"

"Not just you. Did you know that Javi is Patty's grandson?"

This stuns me on more than one level. Javi is so outgoing, and Patty is . . . pretty caustic. "Patty's old enough to have a grandson? I thought she was like thirty-five at most."

Katie uses her hands to pull her skin taut on her face. "Didn't you notice her eyebrows? She paints them on super thick to cover the way her facelift pulled them halfway up her forehead."

"How do you know she had a facelift?"

"Because I knew her before she had it." Katie bites her bottom lip. "I met Patty years ago when William started interning at Velocity."

I don't say anything, but she reads my confused expression.

"It wasn't supposed to be a big deal because it's not like we're close, but William is my cousin."

"But he's—"

"Horrible? Yeah. That's definitely true at the office."

"He calls you Intern."

"He did it to force separation between us, constantly reminding himself that I wasn't the little girl who he used to take baths with."

I gag.

She laughs. "I feel the same way. But then you came along, and he couldn't call me Intern and you by your name, so you got stuck with Coffee."

We fall silent for a few seconds, and thoughts tumble over each other in my head. "Poor Mara. She probably feels like she has no chance."

"Don't feel too bad for her. She was William's girlfriend last summer."

True.

"And he really is trying to be fair," Katie continues, stretching out on the bench and shading her face with her hand. "He even created this spreadsheet, tallying up all of our accomplishments this summer so he knows which intern was the most valuable. So far, I'm at the bottom of the list—and yes, he told me."

Yikes.

"It doesn't matter as much to me as it does to you. My mom just wanted me out of the house doing 'something productive' for the summer and begged William to take me on."

Having more than one avenue to college would be nice. I mean, there's a chance I could have tried out for a university dance team somewhere and gotten a little scholarship money, but it's not the direction I want to go. Knowing the way my brain works means that I'd go to school *and* dance *and* study. Sleeping and eating would happen only when I was done studying, and I learn even slower when I'm tired.

"This is depressing." She tosses her fork into her salad and steals half of my cornbread. "Tell me about Gabe, besides the obvious fact that he's so hot he might melt your face off."

"He's not what I expected." *He is gorgeous and cocky and ridiculously flirty, but he's also sweet and funny and a little bit broken.*

"And an amazing kisser?"

So much that. I take a bite of my macaroni to avoid eye contact. "Who said anything about kissing?"

"Girl. Please. I saw the pictures. The game? Going back to your apartment?"

My lips won't cooperate. I can't contain my smile as that moment on the roof resurfaces.

"Maddie!" She steals the other half of my cornbread. "Do not make me eat this!"

"That is the stupidest threat ever."

She shoves the whole thing into her mouth. "This is what you get for not giving me details," she says, crumbs flying in every direction.

"You're using this as an excuse to cheat on your triathlon diet."

Katie grimaces, her face pinched like she might start crying any second. "I totally am."

My phone buzzes.

"Is it him?" she asks, still trying to choke down the cornbread.

It is. Seeing his name on the screen sends a jolt of nerves through me.

Gabe: Are you telling me no?

Me: Did you send me another text? I missed the question.

Gabe: The charity banquet.

Gabe: Do I need to find another date? It's sort of short notice.

"You tell him yes, right now. Or I will do it for you." She reaches for my phone, but I have the height advantage.

Me: Yes.

Gabe: Yes, I need to find another date? Or yes, you'll come with me?

It might be my imagination, but I swear he sounds a little frantic. There's a naughty part of my brain that wants to keep playing with him.

Me: Yes

Long pause. The three little dots start to cycle, but I send a follow-up message.

Me: I'll go with you.

Katie cheers and then steals my macaroni and cheese. "So what are you going to wear?"

"Oh crap." I put my hand to my forehead. "I need a dress."

Katie grins, one cheek still full of noodles. "You need *the* dress."

Twenty-One

WITH GABE IN NEW YORK FOR A GAME AND THE AUTOMATED system up and running, I have the whole weekend off. Sort of. Early Saturday morning, Emma drags me out of bed for a fancy brunch at Mortar & Pestle, which seems wrong because I'd rather not go dress shopping with a food baby. That doesn't stop me from eating a huge plate of brioche French toast with the creamiest custard in history. Em seems to be enjoying our outing as well. She's buzzy and happy and talking almost as fast as I do.

"Did you have a chance to talk to Gabe before he flew to New York?" She doesn't look up from her plate of blueberry pancakes, but it doesn't feel like a passing question.

"I didn't, but I will when he gets back."

"You need to. Geoff will be at the banquet on Friday night and is expecting to speak with him."

My happy feeling evaporates. "I don't think Gabe will go if he knows Geoff is going to be there."

"Contractually, Gabe *has* to be there."

I put down a forkful of powdered-sugar deliciousness. "Have contracts stopped Gabe from doing stupid stuff in the past?"

Em lets out an irritated huff. "If Gabe will just sit down and talk to Geoff, they'll work it out. Gabe can't burn bridges like this and expect to succeed."

I know she's right, but I also wonder how she can be so willing to help out her ex-husband. It sort of makes me wonder what's in it for her besides being professional. A secret bonus? A promotion? Or maybe something more personal? Whatever it is, I can't imagine that Geoff and Gabe would ever be a good fit as coach and player.

Sort of like me and the Smacker—the ancient ballet teacher that some of the parents at our studio loved because she got great results out of their kids. I was used to getting yelled at by my coaches. Sometimes they even physically corrected an arm or leg placement, but this lady got so frustrated with me that she slapped my thigh to get me to move it. From that point on, I was terrified of screwing up in her class. Instead of the fear making me better, I messed up worse. Finally, I quit ballet and was so much happier for it.

I don't want Gabe to end up hating soccer, but I also don't know that he would hate playing for Geoff.

Emma peeks at her phone and jumps. "Put down that fork. We've got to leave right now or we'll be late for our appointment."

"Appointment for what?"

She beams at me, eyes sparkling with excitement. "You'll see."

WE GET OUT OF THE TOWN CAR IN FRONT OF A STORE I'D NEVER imagined shopping in. I recognize two of the dresses in the window from the tabloids.

I stop on the curb and shake my head. "Em, no. I can't shop here. I don't have that kind of money."

"But I do."

"I could never pay you back."

"I'm not asking for that. All I need is for you to show up at the gala properly attired with a very happy, very reasonable Gabriel Fortunato on your arm."

Animated conversation. Beautiful breakfast. Couture shopping. Anybody smell a bribe? "Why does this feel like you're trying to coerce me into doing something?"

"For heaven's sake, Maddie." She huffs in exasperation. "The gala is in six days. I had to pull *all* the strings to get this appointment, and they will not appreciate us being late."

Em hooks her arm through mine and tows me toward the building. As she swings open the door, the breeze from the air conditioner pushes an amazing scent toward me. Apparently, this bribe smells like jasmine.

"Come on." Her frustration gives way to a real, albeit slightly tired, smile. "This is something I've always dreamed about doing. Don't spoil my fun."

A woman in a gorgeous pantsuit greets Emma with a hug and two kisses, then ushers her toward a white leather chair in front of a wall of mirrors. She has a pompadour, giant diamond earrings, and perfectly winged eyeliner.

"Maddie, this is Thatcher Rouge. She is an absolute genius." She gives me a little push in Thatcher's direction.

"Lovely. Just lovely." Thatcher puts her hands on her hips and walks around me in a circle. "You were right, Emma. Your color palette will not suit her."

She leans close, squinting at my face, and I try not to lean away from her appraisal.

"*Mmmm.* I have the perfect thing." She claps her hands sharply and starts walking away.

"Follow her," Em whispers, as she accepts a flute of champagne from an assistant who materialized out of nowhere.

The dress is red like expensive cars, apples still on the tree, and the lipstick my mother would never let me wear. The wide neckline barely clings to my shoulders, showing off collarbones I sort of forgot I have, then it hugs my body to my knees before flaring out just enough for me to walk.

Thatcher makes it clear that because we're in a time crunch that this is *the* dress. It won't require much alteration, and with the right shoes it won't even need to be hemmed. My mom always says, "You get what you get, and you don't throw a fit." But if she saw the back of this dress—or the lack thereof—she'd throw a temper tantrum to rival the orangutan at the Lincoln Park Zoo. Pounding on glass and slinging poop would have nothing on Mom's rage.

But standing in front of the full-length mirror, with my hair pulled back in a low, elegant bun that Thatcher held into place with a bobby pin that looks like a corkscrew, I'm certain I have made a mistake of epic proportions. This dress is *red*, and my back is bare all the way to my waist; knowing that people will see me makes my skin crawl.

Or maybe that's the plastic, padded bra that's stuck to my body with heavy-duty double stick tape.

"I don't know, Em." I lick my lips, which Thatcher painted with some lacquer the same shade as the dress. It burned like chili peppers and made my lips puff up. Which I guess was sort of the point. "Do you think it's too much?"

"It's exactly what you should wear to an event like this." Thatcher huffs and tucks a strand of hair back into my bun. "Convince her," she commands, before strutting away like a peacock in a tizzy.

Emma sets her champagne flute on the small side table and comes to stand next to me. "Forgive Thatcher. She's not used to being questioned. But if you don't like it or—"

"It's not that I don't like it." I can't look at myself anymore, fingers worrying the seam at my hip. "I just feel . . . *visible*. People are going to notice me."

She takes my hands in hers, and her bottom lip trembles a little bit. "So what if they do, Maddie? What are you so afraid they'll see?"

A totally normal girl. An average girl. A girl stuffed in a fancy dress and in a place where she doesn't belong.

Emma lifts my chin, and there's no questioning the tears in her eyes. "I know you've never felt as smart or as talented as your brother. I know that was never your parents' intention, because they were trying so hard not to compare you two to each other."

Or more likely, they just didn't think I was comparable.

"I need you to wipe all of that out of your head. Book smarts don't come as easily to you as they do to Max. So what? You're great with people. You have common sense. And you work hard for what you want. To me, those qualities are more important than just being smart." One tear drips down her cheek, and her voice gets higher. "I love your brother. He's wonderful. God knows I wish you kids were mine. But your parents haven't done enough, in my opinion, to make you realize how valuable *you* are." My eyes start to burn, and she gives a watery laugh. "Don't cry. It'll make Thatcher angry."

Em fans my face, and I can't stop the snort-laugh. "I'm sorry."

"I'm not sure what you're apologizing for, but my point is that it's okay to be seen. Let Gabe and the team and whoever else is at that gala see how funny and smart and delightful you are."

Funny and smart and delightful. I can be that. I smooth the fabric of my dress over my hips. "I do look good."

A hard "Ha!" bursts out of her mouth. "You're going to be fine, and once people start getting drunk—not you and Gabe obviously—you can disappear. Gabe needs to make an appearance, look happy and sober, and smile for the cameras. Then, you can both leave."

I know she's right. So as long as I don't trip on my entrance or knock over a table or spill a drink on someone, everything is going to be just fine.

She turns me back to face the mirror. "You are so beautiful. Don't be afraid to own it."

I look at my reflection and stand a little straighter. "All right," I say. "I guess we'll take it."

"Hallelujah!" Thatcher shouts, as she rounds the mirrored wall where she must have been listening in. "Don't cry. It'll leave drip marks on the material."

Emma and I look at each other and laugh.

Twenty-Two

THE ENERGY IN VELOCITY IS FRENETIC. WITH THE GALA ON Friday, there are so many tiny details to attend to: name tags, seating charts, printing the forms for the silent auction, putting together the boxes that will hold the raffle tickets, and on and on and on. There are details that I'd never even considered. Like assigning Table Captains—people who are well versed enough in the team's charity to be able to speak about it passionately and coherently.

Gabe doesn't get back until Monday and has practice and team meetings on Tuesday, but we plan to have dinner together on Wednesday at Moretti's.

Just before noon, I get an email that the office is providing lunch in the Lakeside conference room. I expect to poke my head in, grab a box, and go somewhere to eat. When Katie and I open the door, there's no food and the entire staff is crowded around the table. Arman, Javi, and Mara stand along the window. Arman waves, but Javi and Mara are whispering intensely to each other and don't acknowledge us.

I wedge myself between Katie and the suspiciously empty sideboard. "Is this a meeting?" I whisper. "Is the food not here yet?"

"I don't know, but I'm starving." Katie wraps her arms around her middle. "I feel like we're being held hostage."

"From who?"

"From our food."

I have to stifle a laugh as Aunt Emma walks to the head of the table. "I called this lunch meeting today to celebrate something remarkable." She nods to William, who turns on the video projector. A still image of Gabe at the piano fills the whiteboard. Em grabs a red marker from the tray and draws a big circle around the hit count. "This video is officially viral! It's gotten more than 5.4 million hits in the first seven days. And perhaps the most amazing part is that it was conceived, shot, and edited by one of our interns—Maddie McPherson!"

The staff applauds. From across the room, Arman cups his hands around his mouth and yells, "Good job, Maddie!"

And I stand there frozen, cheeks burning, barely feeling Katie's hands pushing me toward the front of the room.

I stumble toward my aunt, who pulls me into a tight hug, and then leaves her arm around my shoulders. "Because of this video's success on multiple platforms, Mr. Fortunato has been invited to play on *Good Morning America*'s Summer Road Trip series, which will be in Chicago on Thursday!"

My mouth drops open in shock as the Velocity staff cheers again. Pride shoots through my veins. I've totally done something right. For once in my life, I set out to do a good thing and everything went according to plan.

"At Velocity, we believe in celebrating each other's victories," Aunt Emma continues, as Patty rolls in a catering cart laden with boxes from the fancy restaurant in the Four Seasons hotel. "Please, eat and enjoy, before we all have to get back to work."

Everyone laughs and then the junior and senior executives—

who have mostly only thanked me for their coffee—come up to shake my hand and tell me what a fabulous job I've done this summer. One even asks if I plan to come back next year.

"Congrats, Mads." Emma pulls me into another hug. "I've already run everything past Gabe, and he's looking forward to it."

The words crack like a wet towel across my back, chasing away my happiness with a sudden sting. "He's looking forward to it? Really? I thought he'd be a little hesitant."

"He knows it will be good for his image and his future." She smiles and tilts her head toward me. "Plus, he knows it will be good for you."

I WORK LATE ON WEDNESDAY AND RACE OUT OF THE BUILDING TO get to Moretti's. It's a beautiful day, the bus arrives thirty seconds after I do, and I get to see Gabe. All good things.

The bus is a little crowded, but even that doesn't dampen my mood. If I were in a musical, I'd do some choreography down the aisle and swing around the pole.

When my phone rings and his name appears on the screen, I almost do.

"Hey! I'm on the bus. Do you think Maria will have risotto again tonight? It's on the menu so I'm assuming she has it every night."

He's silent for a second too long. "I'm so sorry. I haven't left my apartment yet."

"That's okay. I got out of work late." It's like a rain cloud is trying to blot out my sunshine, but I'm not going to let it. "Em told me about the whole *Good Morning America* thing."

A piano key plunks in the background. "Yeah." Then it's painfully quiet. "Good news, right?"

"Do you think it is?"

"Scott and Emma and everyone think that it's a great opportunity, so it must be."

I readjust my grip on the overhead bar, thinking about the other big opportunity Scott and Emma think he should take. Now is definitely not the time to bring it up. "And yet, I'm not convinced that you're convinced."

He plays some chords in the background, and I can't help but imagine him in his too-dark apartment with the phone pinched between his ear and his shoulder, posture curved with unhappiness. "I can't figure out what to play."

While I believe that's part of it, I think he's also worried what people—specifically his family—will say when they see it.

"I can get off the bus at the next stop, pick up some food, and bring it to you." The bus jolts and a crew of people start to spill out. "We can figure it out together."

"Madeline." A hint of humor laces his tone. "If you come over here, I will not be able to focus on the piano."

I flush all the way to my hairline. "That feels like a backhanded compliment."

He laughs, and that heat meanders all the way to my toes. "Just a compliment."

"Fine," I say with a happy sigh. "I'll see you in the morning?"

"Ci vediamo presto."

I don't know what that means in English, but it sounds like a promise.

WE HAVE TO BE AT THE STATION BY 5:30 A.M. EMMA AND I WILL PICK up Gabe on our way, so there's no chance of him sleeping through his zombie apocalypse alarm clock or having his phone die or whatever possible excuse.

By some miracle, he's leaning against the side of his building when we turn onto his street. With his navy pants, emerald green blazer, pin-striped shirt, and a pair of loafers that must be Italian, he looks exactly like a photo from a fashion magazine. Seeing him again sends an electric shock through my body, and all the butterflies in my chest scatter in a spastic flurry.

So much for trying to play it cool.

"Well," Emma says, as she leans across me. "We won't have to dress him for the occasion."

"It's just one more thing that he does well."

Emma looks over at me, eyebrow cocked.

"I'm just saying that he's good at a lot of things," I correct myself, but it makes her bite her bottom lip to stop from smiling. "You know what, never mind."

"Hmm."

The car pulls into the half-circle driveway in front of Gabe's apartment, and he climbs in the front passenger seat. I sort of wish he would have squeezed in the back with us, which is ridiculous. It would have been a tight fit, but it would have given me the perfect excuse to be pressed up against him, to brush my hand against his, to smell that faint woodsy cologne he wears.

I'm wearing a robin's-egg blue sheath dress that makes me look more like a woman than a stick of celery. That was one of the comments from the WAGs Instagram account, and it's unfortunately accurate. The dress hugs my nearly invisible curves. Yes, I wore it with the post in mind, hoping Gabe would notice.

When he looks over the back of the seat, I think he does. "Good morning," is all he says, but the quirk of his lips, the way his eyes linger on me, make it seem like he said so much more.

Emma wishes him good morning—reminding me that we're not alone—and congratulates him on the team's last two victories. He does exactly as he's been trained and comments on his teammates' hard work and their accomplishments, and how well his opponents played. It's polite and to the point, but a little too on the nose. She asks him a few questions from the list *Good Morning America* sent over. It's all the same—canned answers. No personality. No charm. It's like he's reading lines.

"They've set up an open-air studio near Buckingham Fountain," Em explains, leaning forward slightly in her seat. "You'll film the piano piece first and then the interview."

He nods without looking back at either of us.

Em gives me a questioning glance and mouths, "Nervous?"

"He'll warm up," I respond, hoping it's true.

When we reach Grant Park, a white tent is set up on the gravel that surrounds the giant wedding cake–style fountain. Behind that a temporary awning provides shade to the camera crew and anchors without blocking the cityscape rising over the dancing spray. The water reflects the sunrise, gilding the verdigris seahorses at the base. I can see why they chose this location. It's gorgeous.

We're greeted by one of the producers, then whisked into the tent, which is cooled by industrial-sized fans. Emma and I stand off to the side while the hair and makeup crew fawn over Gabe. He turns on the charm under their attention, and the stylist takes extra long fixing his already perfect hair. I'm pretty sure it's an excuse to stay close to him. Jealousy prickles on the back of my arms, but I ignore it.

Finally, they move on to the next guest because, honestly, how much work can you do on a guy who looks like that? Emma is off in the corner talking to someone she knows. Gabe and I are relatively alone for the first time in a week. I slide up beside the tall studio chair they've given him. His right ring finger taps against the chair's arm like that first day in the conference room. It's his tell. He *is* nervous.

I touch the back of his hand, stilling the tapping finger.

His real grin appears—it's sweeter than the one he'd given the makeup artists—and I know it's for me.

"Stop fidgeting. You're going to be brilliant."

"I'm always brilliant."

I roll my eyes at his confidence, but I'm also glad he has it. At some level he struggles with insecurity—just like me, just like anyone—but deep down, I know that Gabriel Fortunato truly believes in himself, in his hard work, in his skill. And, I remind myself, that he'll never achieve his dreams if his insecurities keep him in MLS.

Encouraging him to meet with Geoff is the right thing, but that doesn't mean it's going to be easy for him to hear. "Speaking of your brilliance, Emma and Scott really want you to think about playing for Arsenal."

"Madeline—"

"Hold up. Just hear me out." I slip my fingers between his and hold tight. "I know you have reasons to hate Geoff, but meeting with him, maybe playing for him for *one* season, could be your chance at getting back to European soccer. It could open other doors for you."

He closes his eyes like he's trying to block me out.

"I know you don't want to be *here*. In Chicago. In MLS. But I don't want you to give up on your passion. You love the game so much. You want to play somewhere big, somewhere competitive. So please." I squeeze his hand again but get nothing in return. "Just consider it."

Gabe lets out a long breath before pulling his hand free from mine. "I don't. Want. To think about it." His voice isn't loud, but it's sharp enough to draw the closest hair and makeup team's attention. He notices and stands up, squaring himself in front of me. "I will never consider it. *Please* don't bring it up again."

I look into his eyes and see resolve and a little bit of hurt. Hurt that I caused. "I'm sorry," I whisper, touching his jacket sleeve. "I just want what's best for you."

"Then trust me when I say that Geoff isn't it." He walks toward the refreshment table, but it feels like he's walking away from me.

Emma snags him before he picks up a pastry. "You're up next. This audience is going to eat this up! Everyone is going to absolutely love you."

"Because that's what's important, right?"

She ignores the acid in his voice, brushes lint off his shoulder, and smiles. "Yes, it is. Especially when you're a public figure."

He says nothing, allowing the producers to usher him to the piano, where we snap dozens of still photos of him standing between two of the female hosts. His smile is fake, but I don't think anyone will notice that when I post the pictures as a teaser. Hopefully thousands of people will watch his segment the moment it goes live.

Because that's what we want. Isn't it?

Gabe sits down, wipes his palms on his pants, and begins to play a song from *The Greatest Showman*, but it's not straight off the sheet music. He's mixed in something from a British band I can't name. It's phenomenal. He is such a gifted musician. And athlete.

Both anchors are stunned by his talent and a little bit giggly. They do not stick to the preselected questions we prepped Gabe for.

The dark-haired host leans over the side of the piano, elbow propped dreamily on the side, and says, "Tell me: Is there some lucky girl in your life? Someone who gets to watch you play soccer during the day and fall asleep to music like that at night?"

Gabe gives her his practiced smile, the one that's just a little too dashing to be authentic. "Are you auditioning?"

Everyone laughs. Everyone but me. I stand behind the cameras, watching Gabe play these anchors like he did the piano. He turns up the accent—it usually isn't this heavy—for their benefit. It's another tool in his arsenal of charm. These two older women fall for it and all over themselves for a boy who's barely legal.

I think back to every conversation I had with Gabe, every text, every hand touch and smile, and I wonder if maybe I didn't fall for it too.

"That's not a straight answer," the blond one teases. "You've been linked to dozens of models and designers and heiresses. Is there someone like that in your life?"

My breath catches in my throat, and I wait on pins and needles with the rest of the world to hear his response.

"No," he says, shaking his head, but his eyes land on me. "There's no one like that."

My brain tells me he only said it because he protects his privacy and the people he cares about. But a little corner of my heart— maybe pinched by my own insecurities—is telling me that this is his way of saying there's nothing between us.

AFTER THE SEGMENT ENDS, I RUSH TOWARD THE PARKING LOT, tapping on my phone, cutting and pasting the text that had already been approved for this post. When the car pulls up, I climb inside before the driver comes around to open the door. Gabe must have been right on my heels because he ducks in after me, so I have no choice except to slide across the seat or end up with him on my lap.

Should I ask him what he meant, or would that make me seem stupid? Or clingy? Or needy? I don't want to be any of those things. I just want a clear answer.

But before I can formulate a question, he asks, "How do you think it went?"

Right. Of course he's worried about that. "Good. Really good."

"Good." He nods once, then focuses on his phone.

I wait, hoping for an explanation because this is a perfect opportunity. The driver is outside waiting for Emma; we're alone. When the silence stretches, I guess I have my answer. He's ignoring me in favor of his phone, which makes it pretty obvious that he doesn't want to talk. I turn to face the car window, so I don't have to look at him, so I don't have to notice how his suit jacket makes his eyes more green than hazel. I don't want to think about the night on the roof. I don't want to think about his skin against mine or the way my heart races every time I hear his voice.

Emma climbs in, completely oblivious to the tension in the car. She's thrilled the interview went so well and that both anchors were so charmed by him. "You really have a gift with people. You make everyone believe they're someone special."

That is an understatement.

Twenty-Three

I PICK UP MY PHONE A THOUSAND TIMES ON THURSDAY AFTER-noon, thumb sliding over the keys, drafting an apology to Gabe, then a fake question, then just a hello, but I don't send anything at all. And I don't hear from him, which is worse in all of the ways.

My brain—my relentless, cruel brain—has our entire interaction in the *Good Morning America* tent on repeat. Listening to him tell the anchors there was no one in his life is tied for most mental views with the betrayal on his face when I brought up Geoff.

Friday morning at Velocity is shot. We're all frantically double-checking last-minute details before we shuttle over to the conservatory. Which is sort of a gift because I'm only left alone with my thoughts on the way over. I try to pretend the weight in my chest is heartburn from a Danish pastry I snarfed down instead of heartache. Which is totally ridiculous, anyway. We kissed *one* time. Did I actually expect it to mean something to him?

Yes.

When we pull up in front of the Garfield Park Conservatory, I'm momentarily stunned. I visited the conservatory when I was little, but the only thing I remember was goats. One managed to put its head through the fence, bite my shirt, and refuse to let go.

I tugged and fought with it before finally calling for help. My mom was busy with infant Cube, and my dad had run off to chase Max, so no one noticed that I was being eaten alive by a demon creature. Eventually, a lady with a preschool group helped free me from the jaws of the horrible beast and delivered me to my mother with the hem of my shirt gnawed to rags.

There's nothing in my memory about a massive oblong greenhouse that showcases the sky or lush plants with heady fragrances and an intricate mosaic fountain in all my favorite colors. Nope, Little CalaMaddie was so scarred by the goat encounter that she blocked out the gorgeous immensity of two acres of gardens under glass.

The whole building is open for the guests to tour—including the Fern Room, the Desert House, the Aroid House (which I learn means it's full of flowering plants)—but the auction will be held in the Show House, under a multicolored dome of stained glass. Dinner will be in the attached Horticulture Hall.

The catering company has handled the majority of the heavy lifting, but it takes a while to get the table assignments arranged, the auction laid out, and the intricate details that will make this event something special. By the time we're finished, Mara, Katie, and I have to hustle to get ready in what I think is the bride's room when the conservatory is used for weddings.

"Holy Hot Mama!" Katie catcalls me as I walk out from behind the little partition that was set up for privacy. "Are you taped into the dress?"

"No. Well, not really. It's got these silicon strips that stop it from gaping open on my back."

I catch Mara's eyes in the floor-length mirror. "Did your aunt hook you up with that, too?"

Pretending not the hear the accusation in her tone, I open the little jewelry box that holds my earrings and bracelets. "It was a gift."

"That sounds about right. Your aunt *loves* to give you things you really don't deserve." The bottom of Mara's full-skirted black dress swishes as she heads toward the door.

I have taken so much of her crap without fighting back, without calling her on it. Anger rolls through my body in a hot wave. "What is that supposed to mean?"

She whirls to face me. "Seriously? You think you *deserved* to work on the Fortunato account?"

"That was—"

"This is my third year interning. If anyone earned the right to work on that account, it was me. I did my time getting coffee and making copies and learning from the executives." She grips the door handle so hard I can see her knuckles go white. "And I have enough self-respect to not throw myself at clients so I had some excuse to get on their account."

"I did *not* throw myself—"

"Aren't you supposed to be out there right now, meeting your *date?* Because that's what you are. Not a publicist. Not an intern. You're the next bit of Gabriel Fortunato tabloid fodder. I hope you enjoy your very short time in the spotlight."

With that, she storms out of the room. Katie and I stand in silence until the echo of the slamming door fades.

"You should file a harassment report with HR," Katie says.

"It's not harassment when she's probably right."

"Don't say that. She's a bully. Period. She wants what you have and is trying to make you feel bad about it."

I give a pitiful-sounding laugh, then look down at my hands pressed against my thighs. They tremble a little, but not with anger. Somewhere in the middle of Mara's tirade, I started to wonder if maybe she was right. I had no intention of stealing anything from her or anyone else, but it still happened.

"Just think about it." Katie grabs the box with my shoes and hands it to me. "You better get moving. William will freak if you're not out there soon."

"Yeah." I step into my gold stilettos, barely able to get the strap around my ankle between my shaking fingers and the cut of my dress.

Katie sees my struggle and helps me get the buckle latched. "She's wrong, you know." She gives me her fiercest grin. "You worked harder than any of us."

"Thanks." I try to find a smile for her, but it wavers.

"Now, go! Before William comes looking for you."

AN ACTUAL RED CARPET HAS BEEN ROLLED OUT, LEADING TO THE entrance of the conservatory. Camera crews from the local news stations and the die-hard fan websites line the area beyond the security barrier.

William is just inside the lobby's doors, pacing back and forth when I reach him. "Glad you decided to show up. Fortunato's car is the third in line." He pushes open the door for me. "If you join him as soon as he climbs out of the car, then everyone will assume you're together."

It's too late to back out, too late to fake sick or break my ankle. Tonight, I'm just an intern learning how to handle red carpet events. I shove all my feelings into a tight little package, ignoring the jagged bits of hurt related to Gabe and the serrated corners of Mara's words.

We edge through the reporters and photographers, then William lifts the barricade for me to step under right as the waiting valet opens Gabe's car door.

He pauses to button his jacket and freezes. I watch the shock of my appearance hit him. He jolts like someone punched him in the stomach and he blinks a couple of times like he expects me to disappear.

Nope, the fairy godmother worked her magic.

Okay, fine. It was a favorite aunt with a black American Express card. Either way, I'm not going to poof into a pumpkin or a sooty servant before his eyes.

He holds out his hand. I slide close enough to take it. A camera flashes behind me, and he shakes off his momentary daze.

"I hate this," he mutters.

It takes all my self-control not to roll my eyes. "You look nice, too."

"Dio, Madeline. That's not what I meant." He steps in front of me, hands low on my waist, and I'm sure William is having a stroke on the sidelines. "You look beautiful."

I try not to let his nearness affect my brain, but whatever pheromone Gabe emits is in overdrive. Hazel eyes, olive skin, slightly curly hair. And the suit. I went to school dances with boys in tuxes. This is a different stratosphere entirely: This isn't the kind of ensemble you rent at the local strip mall, and he doesn't smell like too much body spray. There is a hint of something woodsy and spicy blowing in my direction, but it's unquantifiable and even more alluring. I want to press my nose into the side of his neck and breathe deep.

He's just a client. I'm just tabloid fodder.

The words scrape against the inside of my brain, leaving furrows that instantly fill with an angry sort of hurt.

"Don't get too heavy-handed with the compliments," I whisper, straightening his already perfect lapels. "I might get the wrong idea."

William coughs to draw our attention. "Mr. Fortunato, if you'd please?"

Gabe and I walk a few steps, pose, repeat the process. Someone yells, "Hey, Gabe! Who's your date?"

He turns toward the voice, smirk on his face. "She's part of my publicity team. I have to hire people to keep me out of trouble."

The crowd laughs, and I play along, pretending that he's just so funny.

After maybe ten minutes, William herds us toward the lobby, then toward some potted ferns in a corner. I drop Gabe's hand the instant we're inside the door.

"The waiters are carrying around beverages, but none for either of you." William straightens the tie of what is probably his nicest suit. It still seems a little worn for this particular crowd. "Just to be safe, I don't want to see a glass in your hands. With your luck, some-one will take a photo, and even though you'll be drinking water, the media will assume it's a cocktail."

Gabe nods along, but I can tell he's biting the insides of his cheeks to keep from smiling. "I could hide vodka in a water bottle."

I bump Gabe with my elbow, but William ignores the quip. "You and Maddie will be seated at the dry table with the rest of the nondrinkers."

"Where's the fun in that?" Gabe asks, mock affronted.

"He's teasing," I tell William before he can go into cardiac arrest. "Gabe has promised to be on his best behavior."

He turns to me, naughty-sexy grin in place. "Did I promise? I don't remember that at all."

"Coffee?" William snaps, expecting my confirmation.

"I've got it." I loop my arm through Gabe's, dragging him toward the entrance of the aptly named Palm House. Trees with narrow trunks and spiked branches scrape against the greenhouse's roof. Once we're out of earshot, I step away. "Why do you do that?"

"He calls you Coffee."

"It's a joke."

"It's a stupid joke." He sounds irritated and a little protective.

I totally understand the irritation, but the protectiveness throws me a bit. Why does he even care? *There's no one*, his voice echoes in my head.

"Let's find our seats."

Round tables with silk runners and intricate centerpieces fill the space, pressing up against the flower beds full of ferns. Flickering candles, strands of fairy lights, and carefully muted string music make me grateful for Em's choice of dresses. Anything less ostentatious would have stood out in the sea of ball gowns, sequins, diamonds, and one lady in a tiara.

Mara's taking pictures of everything, probably for her portfolio. Arman is helping people find their seats. Katie and Javi are answering questions about the silent auction items. Waiters in white jackets flit between the groups, offering drinks and appetizers.

"I think we're at table nine," I say, pointing toward a table that's tucked slightly off to the side, half-hidden by the ferns that grow along the glass wall.

Gabe takes a few steps in the right direction, then freezes in the narrow gap between two slipcovered chairs. His posture straightens, shoulders rolling back, then he spins to face me.

"Why is he at our table?"

And without looking, I know.

GEOFF IS HERE. HE WASN'T ASSIGNED TO OUR TABLE. I MADE SURE he and Scott were seated as far away from us as possible, but over Gabe's shoulder, I see Scott stand and move toward us.

"Did you know he was going to be here?" Betrayal darts across Gabe's features.

"No. Yes. I can explain. Emma and Scott wanted—"

"Gabe." Scott's voice is too happy, too loud. "Glad you made it."

Gabe ignores Scott completely, eyes focused on me. "You told me you'd never push me into something I'm not comfortable with." Betrayal makes his face goes cold. "I guess you're not pushing, right? You're just nudging me in the direction everyone wants me to go."

"No, Gabe. I didn't know, I mean . . . I thought—"

"I thought you actually cared about what *I* wanted. Not your aunt. Not Velocity. Silly me."

Scott puts a hand on Gabe's shoulder, but he shrugs him off.

"You," he says, and turns to face his agent, "are supposed to work on my behalf."

"I am." Scott looks at me for support, and I hold my hands out to my sides.

Gabe shakes his head once, disbelief shifting to anger. "I made it perfectly clear that I will never play for Geoffrey Jones." His voice is soft, but not soft enough. People nearby are watching, faces alight with interest.

"He's willing to apologize. Give him a chance—"

"You're fired." Gabe says the words calmly, but there's no questioning that he's serious.

Scott is stunned, mouth open, but makes no response.

Gabe turns and holds my eyes for a second. "I trusted you."

"Gabe—"

He brushes past, and when I step backward, my heel snags in

the edge of a tablecloth. The centerpiece tilts, but I catch the vase before it topples to the floor. In the second it takes me to recover, Gabe disappears.

Katie is standing next to the raffle box near the room's entrance, talking to an older woman.

"Excuse me, I'm sorry"—I interrupt—"did you see where Gabe went?"

"Beautiful boy with dark hair?" The woman nods to her left. "Went toward the Show House."

People crowd the two aisles around the central display of flowering plants. I wedge my way between couples, and ask his teammates, members of the Velocity staff, even the waiters if they've seen him. No one seems to know where Gabe went. Dinner starts, my feet are throbbing in my stupid shoes, but he's not at our table or any of the others.

The lobby is empty except for a couple of security guards, and outside the reporters have all left to find a better story.

Gabe's gone.

I call his phone. It goes straight to voice mail. I send a text, asking for him to call me. I get no response. I call again. Nothing.

Dropping to the edge of the low fountain, I put my head in my hands. What just happened? Did Gabe really fire Scott? In front of everyone?

William is going to be pissed. Emma's going to kill me.

But even worse was the hurt on Gabe's face. Hurt I could have prevented. The knife of my mistakes slips between my ribs.

I trusted you, he said. And I betrayed that trust. I should have warned Gabe that we might run into Geoff, but it's such a huge event that I hoped we could avoid him. But I didn't think . . . I. Didn't. Think.

How did I screw everything up so badly?

I try Gabe one more time, then call a cab back to my aunt's apartment, not bothering to tell anyone that I've headed home. It's not like they'd want me around anyway.

I strip off my dress, throwing it across the top of the dresser, and climb into bed still wearing my makeup. Everything hurts worse than it did when I fell off the bike. My head is throbbing. My neck muscles are too tight. But I'd take another gash on my leg over the one across my heart.

Watford hops on the bed and licks my face once before curling up in the curve of my knees. I reach down and smooth his silky ears, and he pushes his head against my hand for more.

He knows exactly what he wants. Food, a soft place to lie, someone to scratch behind his ears. He's loyal and loving and would defend me to his dying breath.

And I hate myself a million times more.

Twenty-Four

EMMA DOESN'T YELL, AND THAT'S WORSE.

She sits on the lavender couch with her elbows on her knees, phone on the coffee table. I sit on the fur rug, hair askew, eyes gritty, and mascara smeared. Watford lies on the floor between us.

"I don't know how to fix this," she says, finally, rubbing her forehead. "Gabe fired Scott. Scott's threatened to fire me. If he does, Velocity will lose a huge account and I'll lose more than just this account. I'll lose my *job*."

She's not exaggerating. Someone filmed the whole scene and sent it to TMZ. The audio isn't great, but the body language is clear. It looks awful. Reporters keep pinging Emma for clarification, but she hasn't answered back yet.

"You were supposed to be on top of this."

"I know. I'm sorry."

"Mads." She covers her face for a moment, then rubs her eyes. "I pulled every string to get you this internship. I talked all the other executives into believing that you were smart enough and mature enough to handle this job."

Oh.

Mara was right to hate my guts. I didn't get this internship on my own merits. It was because I knew the right people. That realization punches the air out of my lungs. I never deserved to be here. "I tried really hard."

"I know. But this . . . is irreparable." She pinches the bridge of her nose like she's getting the headache I already have. "You need to pack."

"What?" The word leaves my mouth with no volume.

"Scott wants you gone. I need to make a drastic effort to keep his business—*to keep my job*—and firing my niece will send a pretty clear message that I'm not going to let anyone mess anything else up for him."

Firing? She's firing me.

Tears fill my eyes, and I don't try to blink them back. "That's not fair. I've worked so hard. I've done every single thing you've asked—"

"I know, Maddie."

"Gabe wasn't—" My voice is high, frantic as I try to make Em change her mind. "I'm not responsible—"

"*You're* the face Scott is associating with Velocity right now." She moves to sit beside me, curling her arm around my shoulders, but I shrug away from her touch. She lets out a long, frustrated breath. "You have to understand. There are so few women in sports business. If I screw up with someone like Scott, I screw it up for all of us."

"Then stand up for me."

"I've already done that, and maybe . . ." She doesn't finish the sentence.

"Maybe, what?" My words are edged with hurt.

"Maybe next year you really will be mature enough to handle a job like this."

She doesn't say my mom was right, but that's exactly what I hear.

I RIDE THE AFTERNOON TRAIN HOME. I DON'T SAY GOODBYE TO ANY-one. Not to Katie. Not to any of the other interns. Especially not to Gabe.

I've lost the faith of two people who mattered to me—one who believed I had potential, and the other whose trust I betrayed.

I choose the quiet car, put my head against the window, and cry. My phone rings once. It's Katie. I wouldn't have answered it even if I'd been in one of the other cars.

Katie sends me a text:

Did you see this?

She attached a picture of me and Gabe outside the banquet. He's looking down at me, eyes intense, mouth soft. If I didn't know how well he could fake it for cameras, I'd almost believe he cared about me.

I delete it without responding.

Chicago disappears and so do my dreams.

Twenty-Five

M Y MOM GREETS ME AT THE TRAIN STATION WITH A LONG hug. She makes me feel like I've been off to war instead of just in the city for a few weeks. "Oh, Sweetie. I'm so sorry this happened." Tears make the mascara drip down the side of her face. "I can't bear to see you hurt."

My swollen eyes start draining again. It's not really crying at this point: Tears are just running without my control.

"Do you want to talk about it?"

"Nope." I bite down so hard on the word that my teeth ache.

She doesn't respond to that, and for once I'm grateful she doesn't try to rub it in or make it worse. Or even try to make it better.

My bedroom feels small and shabby when I get home. I try lying on my lumpy twin mattress, but my body won't let me sleep. Instead, I clean.

I throw away every scrap of old paper. I dig through my drawers, pulling out tights I haven't worn for years and the ballet slippers I grew out of in ninth grade. I make a stack of paperback romance novels to donate to the library. They're all stupid anyway. Who needs some gorgeous, muscly guy to sweep you off your feet? I can say from personal experience it doesn't end well.

My mom comes in and watches. I know she's hoping I'll break eventually and tell her everything. But I've moved from sad to angry. I'm angry at Emma for putting me in this position. I'm fuming at Scott for putting a paycheck over his client's wishes. I'm pissed at Gabe for being . . . Gabe.

When I don't say a word to her, she sends my dad to try. He leans a shoulder against my door frame and says, "Your mother thinks you're going to talk to me. Are you?"

"Not planning on it." I'm not angry at him, but anything I say to him will make it back to Mom.

He's silent for a long time. "For what it's worth, I think Emma was wrong. I understand what she did from a business perspective, but that doesn't make it right."

My eyes well up with tears again, almost managing to push me from angry back to sad. But I hold on to that little ball of anger. It's hot and tight, and so much nicer than the dreariness that accompanies my sadness.

"Thanks," I say as I toss all the paperbacks into a box. "Want to put these in the Goodwill pile for me?"

At some point in the middle of the night, finally tired, I lie down in a pile of old clothes on my bed. Everything went from amazing to awful in a heartbeat. I guess I shouldn't be surprised. This is what I'm famous for—falling down, causing disasters, forgetting, blowing up every important thing.

I really thought this summer would be the end of CalaMaddie McPherson, but it looks like I've just opened another chapter of the never-ending apocalypse that is my life.

The next morning while I'm tossing all my dance trophies into a garbage bag, Max comes in from his night shift at the lab where he works. He lies on my bed, throwing a Nerf football over his head, over and over and over until I can't pretend he's not there.

"Go away, please."

"You're sad."

"I'm not. I'm—" *Tired and mad and hurt and angry at myself.* "I'm nothing."

"You mean you feel nothing? Like you're dead inside?" He stops throwing the ball to look at me.

"No." I feel. I feel so much. "I *am* nothing."

He sits up and drills me in the shoulder with the Nerf ball.

"What the heck? Why did you do that?" I chuck it back so hard that it rebounds off his chest and smashes into one of the dance trophies on the edge of my dresser.

"You are *not* nothing. You worked your butt off this summer. You learned how to edit video and use social media like a boss. You—"

"Screwed up everything? You forgot that part."

He ignores me and pushes on. "You talked to reporters and agents. You set up events. You made a guy who I would generally consider to be a total tool seem like a decent human being." He puts my trophy back on my dresser and pulls down the dance team photograph stuck in the corner of my mirror. "Tell me which one of them could have done everything you did."

I look at the faces of the girls. Some of them I've known since I was three years old, and I tally up their skills. There are some who are smart, some who are organized, some who are outgoing and tenacious.

"I'm sure some of them could." I toss the picture onto my dresser and proceed to tighten all the knobs on the front.

"One of them might have been able to, but you *did*."

"I also messed it all up." My voice sounds watery, and I turn away so that my brother doesn't see my cry.

"No, you didn't. Emma picked the easiest target. This was not your fault. You were in the right place at the right time."

"Or I was in the wrong place at the wrong time."

He sighs. "She might have *said* she pulled all the strings for you, but she wouldn't have done it if she didn't think you were capable."

"But I got fired. I can't put that on my applications to UNC."

"Entrance essays aren't only about your successes. They're supposed to be about what you learned." He opens up my computer and types something into the search bar. "If you want it so bad, don't give up just because it seems out of reach."

"It is out of reach."

"You can do anything. Don't let anyone tell you otherwise."

I shake my head at him. "Come on, Super Genius. That's the best quote you can come up with?"

"Let's see what you can come up with." He grabs me in a head-lock and starts tapping my forehead with his free hand. "Name ten candy bars."

"I hate you."

"That's not a candy bar."

By the time I come up with ten, I'm distracted, my forehead is bruised, and strangely enough, I feel better.

INSTEAD OF DRIVING CUBE TO AND FROM MATH CAMP, HE AND I RIDE bikes. Well, he rides his bike and I carry all his crap while trying to balance on Max's old ten-speed. It's big enough that my knees don't hit the handlebars.

Since I don't have a summer job or dance lessons to teach,

I've spent the last week looking at classes I can take to earn my associate's degree as fast as possible. Apparently, colleges like UNC love to see that students have knocked out all of their generals before they come to school. And then I work on my entrance essay: *Discuss an accomplishment, event, or realization that sparked a period of personal growth and a new understanding of yourself or others.*

I start by writing a timeline, including the bike wreck, which Max insists I keep for comic effect. Putting down everything—how I taught myself to use the video editing software, how I lost the footage, but re-created it, how Gabe's video went viral—it's sort of cathartic. I have a list of real accomplishments, I can clearly see how someone I care about used me to further her career, but I also don't blame my aunt completely. Emma used what tools she had to accomplish a task. It just sucks that I was that tool.

My mom is not one hundred percent on board with my goal of early admission, but my dad finally told her to let it be. And she listened. I can only hope she'll keep listening.

I secretly check the stats of Gabe's games. They lost to Vancouver the day before yesterday, and he got a warning and then later a red. The footage was cringeworthy. The tackle was dirty, and he deserved the card. After the game he had a quick interview, but I couldn't bear to watch it. To listen to his voice and wonder if he's saying exactly whatever his new publicist told him to.

"Look what I can do, Mads!" Cube's little legs pump hard, then he holds his feet far out to the sides, coasting around the corner to our house.

"Be care—"

"Whoa!"

I hear him yell, and I imagine he's crashed over the curb and I'll find him lying sprawled across our grass. Panic makes me pedal faster, shucking safety for speed. When I round the corner, I'm right on at least one account. His bike is on its side in our yard, front tire still spinning.

He's not on it, though. He's standing with his hands on his hips, staring up at Gabe.

I nearly fall off my bike, but I don't because I've been practicing. I hop off in the driveway, parking next to the silver Ferrari. Gabe is answering Cube's questions with a barely hidden smile on his face.

"Is that a real Ferrari?"

"I didn't know there were fake ones."

Cube walks toward the car, eyeing the insignia on the back. "My friend Raj's brother has a Honda with a Mercedes-Benz hood ornament. He found it after a car wreck."

"Did you want to see the inside? It's got the Ferrari symbol on the steering wheel too." Gabe clicks the lock.

"Do not climb in that car, Cube. You're going to get it dirty."

Gabe peers over Cube's head and his eyes catch mine. Seeing him here, having him this close, is like a punch to the gut. It's been easier to convince myself that I'd never see him again. That he'd just be that cute soccer star I knew that one summer I lived in Chicago.

He looks away and smiles at my brother. "It's just a car. I'm not worried about it."

"I am." I grab Cube's shoulder and turn him toward the front door. "Go inside, Cube."

Cube digs in his feet, the grass going flat. He narrows his eyes at Gabe. "Are you the boy that made my sister cry?"

Gabe's mouth falls open. "I—"

"Nobody makes my sister cry." Cube holds up his little fist in threat.

"Oh my gosh. Go. Inside." I give my brother a shove.

He huffs but jogs up the stairs and lets the screen door slam after him. From inside I hear him yell, "Mom! There's a boy here to see Maddie and he drives a Ferrari! I think it's the one who made her cry."

It lifts the weight in my stomach for a moment before it crashes down again. My life is embarrassing enough without my kid brother threatening an international soccer star.

"I'm sorry. He's . . ." I don't have enough words to describe Cube. I take off my helmet and try to smooth down hair, but it's a lost cause. Why am I even trying? Also, why do I care what Gabe thinks about my appearance? I shouldn't. Because we are not and never were a thing. "Why are you here?"

"I needed to talk to you."

"I have a phone."

"Mine's only charged half the time."

"Is that why you never called me back? Or responded to my texts after the gala?" I try to keep my face emotionless, afraid he'll see just how much it hurts to stand this close to him.

He runs his hands through his hair, more frustrated than I've ever seen him. "I didn't . . . I just . . . Look, I talked to Mara."

So much for emotionless. "What? Mara?"

"Yeah. She called and said you'd been fired and—" *wanted to gloat*, my irrational mind suggests before he finishes his sentence. "She felt really bad about how things went down. She said your aunt had her switch the table assignments so that Geoff and Scott were sitting at our table."

Emma. That traitor. A wave of anger hits me so hard that I actually see black. "Then at least you know that I didn't set you up. And . . . and I'm sorry." I set my helmet on the front porch and curl my shaking fingers into my palms. "So, if you drove all the way out here hoping for an apology, then there you go."

"That's not why I'm here." He steps closer to me. "She said you knew Geoff would be at the gala——"

"And I thought we could avoid him. Or make our appearance and leave. I didn't expect him to be *right there*."

"I know." His eyes are wide and earnest, more green than hazel. His usually perfect hair is mussed, and I'm pretty sure he's wearing his workout clothes. Did he come straight here after practice? That's a three-hour drive. I don't let myself imagine him finishing his training, hopping straight in his car, and speeding to get to me as fast as he can. I can't let that information touch my heart.

"Great." There's the chill I was hoping to muster. "I'm glad that's all cleared up. Please go."

I see the frost land on his skin, the cold registering, but he's Gabriel Fortunato. He's not accustomed to being iced out.

"Fine, but let me explain one thing to you first."

"Gabe——"

"I saw the pictures."

"Which pictures? The ones of you storming off?"

He makes an expression like he swallowed something sharp. "Those too, but I'm talking about earlier. The ones on the WAGs account? The one of us at the game? At your hotel?"

The ones with the horrible comments. "What about them?"

"It made me . . ." He clenches his hands like he wants to strangle something. "It made me livid. No one should talk about you like that."

"It's a free country." I shrug like it doesn't bother me, even though it ate at me like battery acid—right up until Em fired me. Then there were bigger issues to be upset about.

"Fine. Freedom of speech. But that doesn't make it okay. I'm tired of my fans threatening the people I care about. After the World Cup, people said horrible things to me. To my family. And then after my car crash, hundreds of people commented that they'd wished I'd died."

Hearing him say it out loud makes me cringe.

"I never wanted anyone to make you feel like those trolls— *Trolls* is the right word, yes?"

It makes me smile, in spite of myself. "Yes."

"I didn't want those trolls to have access to you. It was easier for me to pretend that you meant nothing when really . . ." He steps even closer and touches my arm. "When really you mean too much."

Who knew that such a simple touch could set off a chain reaction of sensation? It starts where his thumb lands on the crease of my elbow, racing up my arm like a lit fuse, and ignites in my chest. "*Too* much?"

"After what I said on *Good Morning America*, I thought it would be easier to let you go." He studies me, lips soft and sad. "I was wrong."

I must have been holding my shoulders by my ears, in a constant protective hunch for days, but his words relax those muscles. "But you were so quiet in the car and—"

"And it hurt." A flicker of pain crosses his face. "I'm so sorry. I was upset and I wasn't thinking clearly and . . . maybe this will help." Gabe reaches into his back pocket and pulls out a slightly crumpled envelope. "I stopped by your office, and that stronzo who calls you Coffee—"

"William?"

"Yes, William." Gabe shakes his head. "I talked to him, and he said he was sorry for the way things worked out and sent you this."

I feel like I'm back at the top of the stairs, barely balanced on the bike, waiting, waiting, waiting for the drop to come. I open the envelope and pull out a one-page letter on Velocity-branded paper.

"Dear Board of Admissions:

I've had the privilege of working as Madeline McPherson's internship adviser for the summer, and I'm happy to recommend her to your program."

William lays out my skills, the traits he found most valuable, and that he looks forward to working with me in the future.

"You talked to William about *me*?"

"I knew this mattered to you." He smooths a strand of sweaty hair off my face, tucking it behind my ear. "And you matter to me."

"But why?" I give a sad-sounding laugh. "I'm not rich or famous. I'm not a model. I'm just normal."

He smiles his real smile—the one that's sweet and vulnerable that he saves for private moments when I'm the only one watching. "No. You're a girl *from* Normal who is so far from normal."

I'm dangling over the drop-off, and my breathing speeds up in response to what's sure to come.

His palms are on my waist, fingers sliding through my belt loops, easing me closer. I wind an arm around his neck and pull his mouth down to mine. He tastes like Gatorade and salt, and it's the best combination I could ever imagine. My heart slams against my ribs exactly the way it did as I crashed down the stairs at the beach.

"Does this mean I'm forgiven?" he asks against my lips.

"Not yet. Kiss me again." He does. And again. And again, until I'm plummeting headlong into a fall I don't want to stop.

EPILOGUE

I SWING OPEN THE DOOR TO A NARROW ROOM WITH BUFF painted walls, basic wood furniture—two raised beds and two desks—and magenta-and-white-zebra-striped curtains framing a window looking out onto a snow-filled quad.

The wall to my left is covered in magenta-colored gingham boards with pictures stuffed haphazardly through the ribbons. Hair products and two jewelry stands fill one desk, but otherwise the room is clean.

"Yikes. Whoa," Mom says, shouldering me out of the way to drop the plastic tote on the room's right side. "Your roommate seems to like pink."

"I guess it's a good thing I went with something neutral." I set down the gray-and-white bed-in-a-bag we picked up on clearance at Target.

"Mm-hmm." She's not really listening, busy squinting at my roommate's pictures, probably trying to deduce which one she is.

Starting school in January instead of in August means that I have some catching up to do. Friends to make. Routines to learn. Classes to find. I hope my roommate—Zaria—will make the transition a little easier. If her personality is anything like her decor, I feel like I'm in good shape.

And if it's not, I'm only an hour from home.

"Should we go back for another load?" I ask, opening the tote Mom carried in, itching to make my own mark on this room.

"Let the boys handle it."

By the time we've slid the bed out from the wall, my dad's in the doorway, huffing and puffing with the majority of my wardrobe hung from fingertips. Gabe's right behind him, boxes stacked high in his arms.

He smiles at me over my dad's shoulder, and I melt like the icicles hanging off the roof outside. In the almost six months we've been together, his real grins haven't stopped being potent, but he has started sharing them with a few more people—specifically Mom and Cube. They've sort of adopted him into our family. It's been good for everyone, except maybe Max, who's convinced he's been replaced.

That's what happens when you go to school across the country, Bro.

Mom, Dad, Gabe, and I work well together, and in less than twenty minutes, the entirety of my life is slipped into drawers and closets. Max and Cube gifted me a bunch of stickable frames for Christmas, and I put up pictures of all the people that matter to me.

There's one of me and Katie in my cubicle. She's the only one of the interns I keep in contact with. Then a row of me and Gabe—all pictures the media will never get their hands on.

The last one I stick to the wall is from Christmas. Gabe is posed between me and Max with Cube peeking over his shoulder like a baby koala. Iliana's face is smooshed in next to Cube's, while Mom and Dad flank the group. Our legs blur together in a smear of matching snowman pajamas. Watford stands in the front wearing a Santa hat and two long strings of drool.

Iliana came with Gabe for all our major holiday celebrations, which gave Cube enough time to develop an adorably ridiculous crush on her. He was heartbroken when she went back to Italy the day after Christmas. Apparently Italians celebrate until January sixth, and the lure of a good party was enough to make her go home.

The only person missing is Emma. It's the first Christmas I can remember her not spending with us, but I hope she's happy in London, where she's opening Velocity's first international office. Watford is staying with my family until she gets settled. Arman and Mara will be joining Em next spring.

I'm thrilled for Arman, but less so for Mara. At the end of the summer Katie found my missing footage. It had been moved to a Tabloid folder, and the last user was MC—Mara Cruz. Maybe she thought I'd find it. Maybe it was just a joke. I've talked to my mom about it, and we've decided that Mara is one of those gray villains—someone you can relate to even though you know their actions are wrong. It was okay for her to make me look bad, but she never intended for me to lose my job. Calling Gabe must have been an attempt at redemption. I still wish I would have taken Katie's advice and filed a complaint. Someone needs to tell Mara that the way she treated me was not okay.

Mom thinks it's great fodder for a romance novel. I told her to go for it.

Em and I talked before she left for the UK. It wasn't an easy conversation, and at least half of that was my fault. I idolized Emma for so long that I couldn't see her faults. She's always seemed to have it all together—the style, the wit, the charisma—that it never occurred to me that her outward persona was very similar to Gabe's camera-ready smile. It's a facade, a really good one, that covers up the flawed person underneath. She was so desperate to succeed that she sacrificed my dreams so she could keep pursuing hers.

I understand it for the most part. Emma needs a job to live, and my future is still fluid. I have people to fall back on and she doesn't. But that also made me realize that I don't have to follow in every one of her footsteps. In fact, I'll probably be happier if I blaze a path of my own.

She did send me a really nice card for my eighteenth birthday and a fat check marked "For College." Even though I didn't get into her alma mater, I did get early admission to the University of Illinois. And the thing is, I'm not even disappointed. It *is* close to home, but not that close. It *is* cheaper—my parents were thrilled that I'll only be taking out loans for in-state tuition. It isn't UNC, but it has an even *better* sports administration program.

"Well . . ." Mom spins around in a circle, taking in my finished room. "I guess that's everything."

Then she bursts into tears.

"I wasn't ready," she says, watering my shoulder. "I thought I'd have at least another year. What am I going to do without you?"

We've had this discussion at least a hundred times. Even though I'm close, it doesn't change the fact that some things are going to be different.

But a good different.

Dad manages to extract me from Mom's grip and gives me a long hug of his own before kissing me on the forehead. "You got this, Mads."

He always knows how to make an impact. His four words have my eyes burning hotter than they did with any of Mom's hundreds.

We walk out to their car, and Gabe and I give my parents each one more hug before they get in their car and drive away.

My heart twists in my chest, hurting and happy all at the same time. Goodbyes are hard. And I know I've got a harder one coming up in a few weeks.

I shiver and Gabe instantly pulls me closer, pressing a kiss to the side of my head. His body is literally hotter than mine—he puts off heat like the radiator in my grandma's kitchen—and I tuck myself under his chin, wondering how many more chances I'll get to do this before he's gone.

The transfer window is open until January 31. I don't understand all the ins and outs of international soccer, but his new agent has a deal in the works. In the next few days, we'll have a clearer picture of which country Gabe will be playing in. None of the options are on this continent.

And it doesn't really matter. We've decided to keep following the fortune cookie's advice and just "go for it" one day, one breath, one heartbeat at a time.

"Do you want to go check out the cafeteria?" He takes my hand, holding me close as we inch across the ice-encrusted parking lot.

"Sure. But it's college food. It's not going to be like Moretti's."

He shrugs, but his feet slide, free arm windmilling. I keep my grip and yank him toward me, but he's heavy and smashes into me hard enough to make the breath whoosh out of my lungs.

"Did I just rescue you?" I loop my arms tight around his waist, keeping his toasty warmth pressed against me.

"It was on purpose," he says, dropping a kiss to my lips.

I don't argue because as he kisses me again, I realize that sometimes the best things are the ones you crash into.

ALSO BY

BECKY WALLACE

AVAILABLE WHEREVER BOOKS ARE SOLD!

Acknowledgments

ACKNOWLEDGMENTS ARE ALWAYS HARD FOR ME TO WRITE, but this one is especially difficult. I finished revising this book during my first round of chemotherapy, and there are so many people who helped me survive this process and get this story finished. They all deserve a very heartfelt thanks.

Far From Normal wouldn't be a book without the insight of my editor, Ashley Hearn. She's pretty freaking awesome. I'm so grateful for her sense of story and the way she helps me flesh out characters and plot points. Big smooshy hugs and a thousand thanks, Ashley!

I'm so grateful to the rest of the staff at Page Street for all their hard work on my behalf. I haven't met Will Kiester, Lauren Knowles, Marissa Giambelluca, Hayley Gundlach, Sabrina Kleckner, Tamara Grasty, Juliann Barbato, or the Macmillan sales team so my hugs might not be appreciated. But if a line in the back of this book isn't enough to convey my thanks, I'm always good for a care package. ;) It's crazy how much effort goes into publishing a book, and I'm amazed and humbled by the slew of talented people who get my work onto shelves. Including—and never to be forgotten—my cover designer, Rosie Stewart. It's thanks to her that my book hops off those shelves into readers' hands.

I have met my publicist, Lauren Cepero, and our Marketing Director, Lizzy Mason, so they'll probably accept a squishy gratitude hug and maybe some Cherry Sours. Thank you for getting my work in front of booksellers, librarians, teachers, Instagrammers, reviewers, bloggers, and book lovers. And I'm so grateful to that long list of people for liking my stories and sharing them with other readers. Thank you, thank you, thank you!

A special thanks to Viktoria and Emanuele Magnasco for Italian translations. Who knew this was where a couple of dance lessons would lead?

Garrett Alwert and Mandy Hubbard champion my stories and have faith in my work. Thanks for believing in me.

I couldn't have finished this book without early readers/ authorly friends: Diana Wariner, Lynne Matson, Lindsay Currie, Jessica Lawson, Lindsay Mealing, and Katie Stout. Thanks for coming on this adventure with me. Sorry for all the ugly versions you read before we figured out how to make it a good story. And to my authorly cheer squad—Kristin Rae, Sara Larson, Katie Purdie, Erin Summerill, Emily King, Lisa Maxwell, Breeana Shields, and Cheyanne Young—I'm so grateful for the positive texts and phone calls. Thanks for keeping me rolling and making me laugh, sometimes with bad karaoke.

My non-writerly friends deserve so much thanks, too! Stacy Sorensen is always the first person who listens to my crazy story ideas. This book is as much hers as it is mine. Jen Wegner read an early version and told me it was the best thing I'd ever written, and it pushed me to make it better. Kara McCoy, Caroline Lund, Jen Mortensen, and so many other women encourage me to keep writing even when it gets hard. Thanks, Ladies. I couldn't do it without you.

Now for my family, who always come last in the acknowledgments because they're the most important. My kids are wonderful little humans—Gavin, Laynie, Audrey, and Ady—and are willing to share me so I have time to write. I'm always proud of them, but it's pretty amazing that they're proud of their "Author Mom." I love you punks. To my parents and siblings, y'all got a couple of paragraphs dedicated to you in my last book. You know exactly how grateful I am. And if you don't, it's a lot.

To my in-laws and outlaws, thanks for so much help this year. The Wallaces and Stewarts (Rick, Olivia, Brandon, Elizabeth, Bailey, Benson, Pippy, Jarod, Brianne, Isaac, Jake, Zeke, and Little Liv) are a blessing. My sister-in-law, Elizabeth Wallace, is a saint. She fed me mints and changed ice packs on my hands and feet during chemo appointments. I don't have enough words or pages to express my gratitude.

And last but not least, so many thanks to my husband, Jamie. Thanks for taking this journey with me. The road has been bumpy, but it's never been lonely. Love you forever.

About the Author

ECKY WALLACE IS THE AWARD-WINNING AUTHOR OF *Stealing Home* (Page Street), *The Storyspinner*, and *The Skylighter* (S&S/McElderry). She's a sucker for slow-burn romances, near-miss kisses, and ordinary people doing extraordinary things. Becky worked for a minor-league baseball team, edited a sports marketing magazine, and toured internationally as a ballroom dancer before settling down in Houston, Texas, with her husband, four children, and one very fluffy puppy.